CHECK OUT THESE OTHER GREAT BOOKS BY MZ. BIGGS:

See What Had Happened Was: A Contemporary Love Story (Part: 1-3)

Yearning For The Taste of A Bad Boy (Part: 1-3)

Dirty South: A Dope Boy Love Story (Part: 1)

Falling for A Dope Boy (Part: 1-3)

Feenin' For That Thug Lovin' (Part: 1-3)

A Bossed Up Valentine's (Anthology)

Jaxson and Giah: An Undeniable Love (Part: 1-2)

Finding My Rib: A Complicated Love Story (Part: 1)

In love With My Cuddy Buddy (Part: 1-2/Collaboration)

Your Husband's Cheating On Us (Part: 1-3)

From Cuddy Buddy To Wifey: Levi and Raven's Story (Standalone/Collaboration)

In Love With My Father's Boyfriend (Standalone)

Your Husband's Calling Me Wifey (Standalone)

She's Not Just A Snack... She's A Whole Buffet: BBWs Do It Better (Standalone)

Blood Over Loyalty: A Brother's Betrayal (Standalone)

Married to the Community D (Part: 1-2)

Downgraded: From Wifey to Mistress (Part: 1-3)

A Mother's Prayer (Part: 1-2)

Heart of A Champion... Mind Of A Killer (Standalone)

Turned Out By My Husband's Best Man (Standalone)

Ain't No Lovin' Like Gulf Coast Lovin' On The 4th of July (Novella)

This Is Why I Love You (A Novella)

The Hood Was My Claim To Fame (A Novella)

A Killer Valentine's (Anthology)

Bouncing Back After Zaddy Gave Me The Clap (Standalone)

Tantalizing Temptations in New Orleans (An Erotic Novella)

Santa Blessed Me With a Jacktown Boss (Novella)

Diamonds and Pearls (Standalone)

Dating A Female Goon (Standalone/Collaboration)

Pregnant By My Best Friend's Husband (Part: 1-2)

Wifed Up By A Down South Boss (Thug Love Collection)

Creepin' With The Plug Next Door (Part: 1-3)

Creepin' With My Co-Worker (Part 1)

Crushin' On A Dope Boy: Cashae and Tay (Box Set)

The Autobiography of A Boss's Wife (Collaboration)

Scorned By The Love Of A Thug

The Thug Is Mine (Part:1/Collaboration)

Every Dope Boy Got A Side Chick: Kenyon & Milani's Story (Box Set)

A Boss And A Hood Chick (Part: 1-3)

Yo' So-Called Bae Creepin With Me (Part: 1)

YO' SO CALLED BAE CREEPIN WITH ME 2

MZ. BIGGS

Yo' So Called Bae Creepin With Me 2

Published in the United States of America.

Published by Cole Hart Signature, LLC.

Mailing List

To stay up to date on new releases, plus get information on contests, sneak peeks, and more,

Go To The Website Below...

www.colehartsignature.com

AUTHOR'S NOTE:

Please take the time to leave an honest review on either Amazon or Goodreads after reading the book. Your support is greatly appreciated. Also, feel free to reach out to me anytime via the contact information listed below. Happy Reading...

-Mz. Biggs

Want to connect with me? Here's how:

Email: authoress.mz.biggs@gmail.com
Twitter: @mz_biggz
Instagram: mz.biggs
TikTok: @mz.biggs
Goodreads: Mz. Biggs
Facebook: https://www.facebook.com/authoress.biggs
Author Page: https://www.facebook.com/MzBiggs3/

Look for my Reading Group on Facebook:
Lounging with Mz. Biggs

WHERE WE LEFT OFF:

KAYSON

Toccara was still being distant with me because of the situation with Bree. I wanted to shake her and tell her that she had everything wrong, but I didn't. I was taking Kyson's advice and making her miss me. I came to work daily, smelling and looking good. I could see her drooling over me. When she did try to make small talk, I'd make sure the conversation remained about work. She'd smack her lips and roll her eyes at me, but I didn't acknowledge it, even though I saw everything that she'd done.

Today, was no different. Since Bree was terminated, I'd given Lauren the key to handle things. I was supposed to be interviewing a replacement, but I didn't feel like dealing with it, so Toccara and Lauren were supposed to do it. I slept in a little this morning because I had a headache. Kyson kept me up all night whining about Mone't and wondering if she was okay. It got to the point that I told him to pull up on her. Shit, if she wasn't answering his calls or texts and he really wanted to know how she was, then all he had to do was pull up. I knew that she was staying with Toccara since all that shit went down because she told me when we met up so I could offer her the services of my attorney to make sure Jared and Bree went to jail behind what they did to her. Jared for the unlawful recording, and Bree for revenge porn.

"Good morning, Kay," Lauren greeted me when I finally arrived at work. Toccara stood there, not saying a word. Since she didn't say anything to me, I didn't say anything to her.

"Good morning, Lauren. How are you today?" I made sure to say Lauren's name so that Toccara wouldn't mistakenly think I was talking to her ass.

"I'm good, and yourself?"

"I can't complain. Glad to be among the living," I joked.

"You so funny, Kayson. Let me get back to work. Have a good day," she advised me.

"You do the same," I returned and continued on to my office.

Opening my office door, I was shocked to see that the lights were off. I never turned my office lights off because I didn't want any surprises. Flicking them on, I was surprised to find Bree sitting behind my desk, naked, with her leg cocked up and her hand massaging her pussy. Immediately, my dick bricked up in my pants.

"What the hell are you doing in here?" I fumed. "I know I fired your ass. How did you even get in?" I queried.

"I made an extra key. I knew there was going to be a time when you smartened up and fired me, so I made about three or four copies of the key to the building. It was never my intention to let you go that easy."

"Is everything okay?" Lauren asked, startling me. She began walking toward me, and I threw my hand up to stop her. If she would've reached my doorway, she would've been able to see Bree, and I didn't want her to see that. It would only be something else for her to gossip to Toccara about, and I'd never hear the end of it.

"Yeah, it's fine. Get back to work," I ordered and stepped inside my office, shutting and locking the door behind me.

"Come on, Kayson. You know you miss this," Bree teased. It wasn't that I missed her or her pussy. It was that I was stressed out, and there was no better way for me to relieve the stress than to bust a nut.

"Fuck it," I said and undid my pants. I moved over to where Bree was and leaned over her. "This is the last time."

"Okay, baby. This the last time," she nonchalantly stated.

Pop... Pop...

Popping her hand, I waited for her to move it out of the way so I could dive in.

"Don't be rough, Kayson. I'm still in pain," she voiced.

"Then you need to get the fuck out of my face. If you can't handle this dick, then you don't need to be here," I sternly stated.

"Fine. But not too ro—"

I didn't bother to give her enough time to finish her statement. I slid my dick right on inside of her as far as it would go. She wanted me to be gentle, but that wasn't going to happen. I was stressed the fuck out because of her, and she was going to feel that shit.

Bree and I hadn't been going at it a good ten minutes before we were interrupted. It was a sign that I really needed to leave her ass alone.

"Kayson, I'm still mad at you, but we gotta go. Kyson has been trying to get in touch with you. Mone't has been arrested, and the police are coming for me ne—"

With the front door locked, Toccara came in from the back door. She started talking before I was in her eyesight. She was in awe when she saw me squatted down and drilling inside of Bree while she occupied my office chair.

Immediately, I got up and tried to go after her, but my pants were wrapped around my ankles, and I couldn't move fast enough. I face-planted right in the middle of the floor. Bree used that as a way to get back at Toccara.

Standing from where she was in the chair, she called out to Toccara.

"Aye, bitch..."

WHERE WE LEFT OFF:

Toccara stopped moving and turned around slowly. She moved in closer to Bree, who was still standing there naked. She had a wicked grin on her face. I shook my head because I knew she was begging for another ass whooping.

"I got your bitch, bitch," Toccara spat.

"I only have one thing to say to you," Bree commented.

"You ain't got shit to say to me, because I don't want to hear it. I don't entertain bitches that ain't on my level."

"Awwww... You're mad? Are you big mad or nah?" Bree taunted.

"Fuck you!" Toccara snapped.

"You can't fuck me, but he can. Don't get mad because yo' so called bae creepin' with me, sis," Bree bragged and laughed.

The expression on Toccara's face let me know that Bree had fucked up. She must've caught on to it too because she grabbed her clothes and took off running out of my office.

"Call 911! She's trying to kill me!" Bree yelled. Toccara took off her lab coat and ran after her. Once she caught Bree, it was too late.

TO BE CONTINUED...

1

TOCCARA

The only thing I saw was red. I'd told Kayson that I didn't want him to go outside the lines of professionalism until he could get over whatever he had going on with Bree. That didn't mean that I wanted him to continue to sleep with her. He should've been reassuring me that he was done with her. That must've been asking for too much because he was still fucking the bitch. He was another LeBron. It was crazy how I told myself that after LeBron I was going to focus on getting through my residency and leave men alone for a while. Things were different when I laid eyes on Kayson. I'd heard so much about him and done a lot of research on him that I really began to adore him. Had I known that he was a male whore, then the thought of being anything other than colleagues with him never would've crossed my mind.

There I was in another bad situation. Bree was shooting off at the mouth. That made matters ten times worse. There was no way she was going to get away with it. Mone't and I had beat her ass once, so it wouldn't take much for me to do it again. She took off running, but I used to run track in high school and college, so I was hot on her ass.

Bree had made it to the door and was trying to get out when

I made it to her. She couldn't get out the door fast enough, because she bumped into some man. From behind, he looked quite familiar to me.

"Watch where the hell you're going!" he yelled at her.

"My bad," she replied and continued to run.

As soon as I heard his raspy voice, I knew exactly who it was.

"Stop her!" I yelled, and he reached out with his long, Incredible Hulk–like arms and grabbed ahold of her.

"Let me go," she screamed, but he only gripped her tighter.

My heart raced. The only thought in my mind was to pounce on her. She'd asked for everything I was about to give her. Bree stood there trying to fight LeBron to break free, but nothing she did worked. Grabbing ahold of the long ponytail she'd put in her head, I wrapped it around my hand until I felt her scalp. Moving her closer to me, I balled my other first and prepared to punch her in the face until I heard...

"Freeze." That was exactly what I did. "Let go of the weave and put your hands in the air. Move away from the girl very slowly." Peeking out the corner of my eyes, I was surprised to see two cops standing in the pharmacy with their guns aimed at me. I knew they were coming, but I didn't think they would pull their guns on me.

"Am I under arrest?" I asked them.

"Are you Toccara Jones?" one of the officers queried. He appeared to have some sarcasm in his tone, which I hated. He had a smart-ass mouth. I knew I was going to have to cuss his rabbit ass out.

"Yeah. Now answer my question," I demanded.

"We do have a warrant for your arrest. Please do what we say in order to avoid making matters worse for yourself," he instructed me.

Hearing him say that I had a warrant for my arrest didn't make the situation better. If I was going to jail, I was going to jail for a crime that I actually committed. Not some bullshit ass charges that I was sure Bree made up with her lying ass.

"That's all I needed to hear," I told him before ramming Bree's head into the shelf with the animal crackers. If she wanted to act like a donkey, I was more than prepared to reintroduce her to the rest of her family.

"Come on, Toccara. You're going to get arrested," LeBron pleaded with me.

"They... Are... Going... To... Take... Me... To... Jail... Anyway..." I stated to him, being sure to hit Bree's head against the shelf between each word. My breathing began to slow as I found myself becoming more and more out of breath.

"Ma'am, stop! We are going to have to tase you if you don't," the officer warned me.

"Please, Toccara. Do whatever they tell you to do. I'll bail you out or whatever I need to do to get you out of this. Come on, baby. I love you," LeBron encouraged me. Other than the fact that breathing for me started to become difficult, hearing him say that was the only reason that I got off Bree's ass.

Gradually, I walked upon LeBron. He had a worried expression on his face. It was sickening how much of a pussy he seemed in that moment.

"What's the matter? Why are you acting like a bitch?" I confidently asked him. Using my right hand, I turned it over and used my palm to gently stroke the side of his face.

"I'm not scared. I'm worried about you. I've never seen this side of you before," he replied.

"You've never seen this side because you never did anything to see this side of me when we were together. That lil' lying shit you pulled was enough for me to walk away without catching a charge. You aren't worth my time or energy."

"You know you still love me. I'm the only one that can get you out of this shit, and you know it."

Smack...

"Boy, fuck you," I spat before refocusing my attention on Bree. She was cowering down on the floor. I reached down and grabbed her by the hair again. Continuously, I used my fist to pound her in the face. Blood began to spew from her nose and mouth.

Click... Click...

The sound of the officers preparing to shoot was all I needed to hear.

"Listen to them, Toccara. They will kill you." At this point, I wasn't even sure why LeBron was still talking to me or why he felt the need to tell me that because once I heard the guns being prepared to sound off, I had every intention of doing what they asked me to do. I wasn't a fool by any means. I'd seen more than enough stories on the news where MY people were being executed for no reason. I didn't want to be another statistic.

"I'm letting her go," I informed them, unraveling my hand from her hair. "I'm lifting my hands in the air. I'm unarmed," I continued to talk. I let them know my every move so they wouldn't think I was trying to do something out of line. My movements were as slow as possible.

"That's what I thought. Take your hands off me," Bree spat. Staggering, she stood from where she was on the floor and turned toward me, placing her hands over her hips. Blood dripped from her face, yet she wore one of the ugliest grins that I'd ever seen in my life.

"Toccara Jones?" one of the officers called my name.

"Yes?" I said above a whisper, my eyes darted to the floor.

"Let me officially tell you that you are under arrest," he stated.

"For what?" LeBron chimed in as if he didn't hear the man the first time he said he had a warrant. My mind pondered over how the police found me. Lauren wouldn't have called them because she hated Bree as much as I did. Mone't and Kyson would've never sent them to my job. Kayson was the only person left. That meant that he was on Bree's side. LeBron being there meant that he was on my side. Even though I couldn't stand his ass, it was better to have him on my side than to be left feeling alone. That was if he decided to still be on my side after I slapped spit from his mouth. He deserved that shit though.

"What did I do, Officer?" I innocently asked. I only did that in case there was a chance for me to claim mental insanity later. There was no reason for them to come after me other than Bree reporting that Mone't and I had beat her ass. She talked all that noise only to end up being a scary bitch in the end.

"We have a warrant for your arrest for the assault of Sabreenacle (pronounced Sa-bree-nacle) St. Clair," he informed me.

"For who? What kind of ghetto name is that?" I remarked, causing the officer to chuckle a bit.

"Shut up. Laugh now, but I'll be laughing later. I'm pressing charges and won't be dropping them for anybody. Not even Kayson."

"Honey, I don't care one way or another. Kayson has shown his true colors, and I'm a firm believer that when a person shows you who they are the first time to believe them."

"I tried to warn you, but you didn't want to listen. Kayson has and always will be mine. He can say that he isn't all he wants. We both see now where his loyalty lies."

"No worries. I don't want him. You can have his musty-dick ass. I have bigger fish to fry."

"What is that supposed to mean?" she queried.

"Officer, I'd like to press charges on Tabernacle as well," I commented.

"On who?" the officer asked.

"Tabernacle St. Clair. I want to press charges on her because she hit me first. I hit her in self-defense."

"Be quiet, Toccara. You're admitting that you did assault her," LeBron advised me.

"No, I'm admitting to self-defense. If she would've kept her hands to herself, then I never would've blessed her with these holy hands. Besides, what's there to admit when they saw me whooping her ass like a savage?" It was bad that I was making a joke of the situation. That was all I could do. Sometimes you have to laugh to keep from crying, right? Bree was putting me in a bad position with this bullshit. All over some dick I never even had. At this point, I was sure I didn't want it at all. Not if it was going to have me running around like I'd lost my mind. It was almost as if she was willing to lose her life behind him.

"My name is Sabreenacle, bitch. It's a name you better never forget because when I'm done with you, all the little shit you tried to do in life will be in vain," she taunted.

"Mr. Officer?" I said to the officer. "Sir, if I'm going to get arrested, please let me have a real reason to be arrested. What I did to her was nothing compared to what I could do to her. You see how she keeps talking shit and taunting me, right? She's literally begging me to blaze her ass up," I seethed.

"Well, if that's not the worse you could do to her, then we definitely can't let you touch her again. She'd be dead. You damn near beat her into a coma. I'm not even sure how she's still talking shit right now," he replied.

"Well, I hit her because she hit me. That's self-defense. I guess we both going to jail."

"Did anyone witness her hitting you?"

"LeBron, tell them what you saw. You do owe me that much since the truth was something I couldn't get out of you."

LeBron was hesitant. His dark eyes stayed trained on me as he contemplated what he wanted to do.

"LeBron!" I screamed his name. If he didn't side with me, I was beating his ass too.

"Uh... Yeah. Yeah, I saw the little gremlin-looking girl hit Toccara and take off running. She bumped into me and stumped on my big toe in the process of trying to get away and kept trying to run. I grabbed her because I'm also willing to press charges on her for bumping me and knocking me into the shelf. I'm sore and have a bruise," LeBron lied. "And before I forget, she made threats too," he continued.

"Threats? What kind of threats?" Bree hollered. Her mouth was damn near dragging the floor in shock.

"Like I said, she made threats. She said she was going to kill Toccara. Then she said she was going to kill herself by swallowing a bunch of dicks or something," LeBron alleged. I wanted to laugh at how he was overdoing it. He was retarded as hell for saying that she wanted to swallow a bunch of dicks. She was a pro at that so I was sure that would be the last thing to kill her.

Kayson remained in the same position the whole time everything was happening without having a single word to say. The officers attempted to ask him if he witnessed anything, and he shook his head no. The way he was acting, one would've thought he was a mute.

"Kayson, you've got to help me. Why aren't you saying anything?" Bree cried out for his help. It was useless because he wasn't saying a word.

"You might as well let it go, boo," I joked. "He's not going to say anything because he doesn't want to say or do anything that could incriminate him. There you were trying to fight for a man that wouldn't dare fight for you. I'd feel like shit if I were you," I hinted to her.

"Bitccchhhh..." she snapped and forcefully tried to run toward me. She looked pitiful. Clearly, she was in a lot of pain. That should've been more than enough for her to sit down somewhere, but it wasn't. She was begging for more. The officer that had been barking out orders to me wrestled her down to the ground and handcuffed her before she touched me. He was smart enough to realize that whether I was cuffed or not, if she touched me, I was going to mule kick her ass and stomp the yeast infection out of her.

"Checkmate, hoe!" I expressed as the other officer cuffed me. They quickly carted us out to the squad cars. They had sense enough to make sure we were placed in two separate cars. Both LeBron and Kayson stepped outside with us. They were standing by the car I was in.

"Don't worry about a thing, Toccara. I'll meet you down there with an attorney and get you out of there in no time," LeBron informed me. He'd hurt me, true enough, but what he'd done to help me put him on the road to redemption. If he and his attorney could get the charges against me dropped so I could continue to have a clean record, I'd at least owe him the chance to hear him out.

"No, you will not. Toccara is my woman, and I'll be there to help her out. Your services are no longer needed here. You may leave." Kayson finally had something to say. It was the wrong time to be saying it. When he should've been speaking up for me, he had nothing to say.

"I don't know who you think you are or who you're talking to, but please don't come for me. I'll never walk away from Toccara," LeBron aggressively told him.

"Neither will I. Who the hell are you anyway?" Kayson muttered. He moved in a little closer to LeBron.

"I'm the man she's been with for almost a year. Who are you?" LeBron fired back. He wasn't backing down from Kayson. He balled up his fist and spoke through clenched teeth.

"I'm the man of her present and future. That means that you can dismiss yourself. I can take care of her. Leave before I have you arrested for trespassing," Kayson threatened LeBron.

"Kayson, you had nothing to say up until now. You made it clear to me that you're rocking with Bree. Keep it that way," I chided. I turned my head away from him to avoid looking into his beautiful brown eyes. Doing that would break me, and I'd allow him to win me over. I couldn't do that, because of what he'd done.

Seeing Kayson inside of Bree made me sick. It wasn't the first time I'd seen it. One would think I'd be okay with it. There was a difference. The first time I saw them together, Kayson and I weren't trying to see what could happen between us. We'd taken things to a completely different level since then, and he told me that he wasn't interested in Bree. Yet he showed me time and time again that when it came to her, he couldn't keep his hands to himself.

"Toccara, let me help you. It's not what you were thinking when you saw me with Bree. I was vulnerable because of everything that has been going on. I'm sorry. Let me help you," he pleaded with me.

"You can sit this one out. LeBron got me. Ain't that right, bae?" I queried, being funny. I knew that Kayson hearing me call LeBron that was going to get under his skin. After the way I felt when I saw him with Bree, I wanted to do more than get under his skin. That would possibly happen in due time.

"You on some tit-for-tat type shit, Toccara? You going to run back into this chump's arms? That's foul as fuck. You only doing that shit to hurt me. If that's what you want, then you win. This shit is killing me. Give me a chance to make this shit right, baby. Please," he continued pleading with me.

"You mean the way that you ran back into Bree's arms when you were supposed to be cutting things off with her so we could see if there was anything between us?"

"I told you it's not what you think."

"We've heard enough. You two are going to have to find another time to discuss that shit," the officer quipped. I hurried to shut my mouth so he wouldn't say that I was resisting or not listening to him or whatever trumped-up charge he could try to hit me with. On the other hand, Bree was going off on the way Kayson had switched up and was giving me all of his attention. The only reason I knew she was going off was because they had yet to shut the doors on the cars we were in. I really wanted to tell them to hurry up because the quicker we made it to the police station, the sooner I'd know what the charges were going to be and what I would have to do to get out.

The only thing I could think about was how I was going to call my parents and let them know what happened. They were going to be disappointed in me. That was the one thing I'd prayed I'd never have to do—disappoint them. Kayson wasn't my man, and already, he was costing me a lot. I wasn't sure what was worse—thinking he was this great man and finding out that he wasn't or that I was really considering giving myself to him in the near future. As with LeBron, I was glad I found out about him and how he was before it was too late. Something about relationships was hurting me. It had me wondering if relationships should be off the table for me. Period.

2

KYSON

It had been a few hours since Mone't had been arrested. The only thing I wanted to do was kill Jared and Bree because I knew they were behind the shit.

"What the hell!" I exclaimed when I noticed Bree being brought inside the jail. Toccara wasn't too far behind her. "What the hell happened? Why are you both here?" I questioned Toccara. I wasn't worried about Bree's bald-headed ass. She talked shit all day, every day. The minute somebody fed into the shit and she got her ass beat, she wanted to cry wolf. That was the weakest shit I'd ever seen in my life.

"Well, you already know she called the police and told them that I attacked her. When they came to pick me up, I told them that I hit her ass in self-defense because she hit me first. LeBron vouched for me and said he saw everything. That's why we are both here," Toccara rattled off. "Besides, I caught your brother inside the bitch again, and I had to beat her ass for real. They saw me trying to beat the brakes off her, so I have to deal with the consequences from that too," she added.

Out of everything that she said, the only thing I was concerned with was the nigga's name that she mentioned.

"LeBron? Who the hell is LeBron? Where were you at

when it happened? Have you spoken with Kayson?" I began firing off all types of questions that she didn't have time to answer because they carried her on to the booking area of the jail.

Immediately, I took my phone out and dialed Kayson's number. He and Toccara weren't on the best of terms, but I was sure he'd want to know what was going on with her. If he didn't already know.

Ring... Ring... Ring...

The sound of a phone ringing when I dialed his number caused me to briskly turn around. When I laid eyes on Kayson, he looked like a nervous wreck. His hair was all over his head, and his clothes were hanging off him. I hadn't seen him like that in a while. It had me wondering what went down that I wasn't aware of. Along with Kayson came walking some other big buff nigga. They looked like they were enemies. That was something I didn't understand. Kayson wasn't the type of man to have enemies, so why did this nigga appear to have a problem with him?

"You good, bro?" I asked him when he got close enough for me to whisper to him. We couldn't talk too loudly, because we couldn't say anything that would make the girls look guilty.

"Hell no. Toccara trying to play me."

"Huh? What you mean?" I was lost. Nothing he said made sense. Toccara didn't even seem like the type of person to play anybody. He was leaving out a lot. "Start from the beginning and tell me what happened," I ferociously barked. Kayson was making dumb moves. He and I both could see that Toccara was the woman for him, but he was letting his lust for Bree's good-for-nothing ass put him in a place to potentially lose Toccara for good. I'd be surprised if she was still willing to deal with him after this.

"You know how vulnerable I can be at times, and you know how Toccara had been on that hard to get shit since we left Jared's house. Bree was in my office when I got there today. She was sitting behind my desk playing inside that fat ass pussy of hers. You know I couldn't help but to dive in."

"You did the shit at work? The place where you knew Toccara would be? How stupid can you be? You were begging to get caught," I concluded. It was probably harsh of me to say to him. Kicking him while he was down was the last thing I wanted to do. However, he had to know the truth.

"I wasn't thinking straight. It really just happened. If I could take it back, I would. I swear I would. She won't even believe me when I tell her that Bree doesn't mean anything to me."

"Can you blame her? You keep telling her one thing, but you're showing her something completely different. You can't keep telling her that Bree doesn't mean anything to you, yet you keep running to her rescue or getting caught with her," I scolded him.

"I know. It was stupid. I get it! That's why I need to get her out of here so I can make this right. There's something special about her. I don't want to lose that. I won't lose that. Not if I can help it."

"She's not going to forgive you, so you might as well let it go," the big, tall nigga that walked in with my brother stated.

"Bruh, who the hell are you?" I asked him. He was all in our business, and I didn't know him from a hole in a wall.

"I'm LeBron. I'm here to get Toccara out," he informed me. He had the nerve to stick his hand out and try to shake mine.

Whap...

Hitting that nigga's hand hard as hell, I walked up in his personal space. Kayson was the type of nigga that would argue before fighting. I was completely different. Disrespect wasn't something tolerated by me. That meant this clown had one more time to say something I didn't like, and Mone't and I would be sharing a bunk. He had me so fucked up!

"Kyson, if you ever shake that nigga's hand, I'm going to end up behind bars with the girls," he said to me before turning to LeBron. "Nigga, you need to put your shit back in your pocket before I knock that bitch off your arm," he fussed. My eyes bucked at what the hell was going on.

"I know you just saw me knock his shit out of my way. What I don't understand is why we are beefing with this nigga. I've never seen him before a day in my life. What am I missing?"

"He's Toccara's ex. He thinks he's going to come back and take her from me. That's not about to happen. If I have to beat his ass every time I see him, he's going to know that Toccara is marked territory," Kayson went off. That stunned me. I'd never seen him react with so much passion for any woman in his life before.

"Then what is he doing here?" I asked, still clueless as to why dude was still standing in our face.

"I don't even know what the hell he was doing at the pharmacy."

"I'm the pharmaceutical rep that you were supposed to meet with. I entered the pharmacy right as everything was happening. No, I didn't know that Toccara worked there, and no, I'm not leaving until I know that she's out of here. For you to claim to be her man, you sure did do a piss-poor job at protecting her. Do you know how much trouble she could get into over this if you can't get your lil' ugly ass girlfriend to drop the charges against her? She worked hard as hell to get to where she is. I'm not saying I did right by her. However, I can assure you that I never put her career at risk. Do you really believe she's going to be willing to forgive you after this?" LeBron had a point. This was going to be a lot for Toccara to have to deal with. Like I said, it would be really surprising if she decided she was going to give Kayson another chance after all of this.

"Nigga, shut your punk ass up. Toccara isn't going back to you. Don't stand here trying to preach to me about what I did when you fucked up too. No sin is better than the other, right? Go re-read your Bible, preacher boy," Kayson taunted him.

"And you think she's going to take you back? At least she never caught me with another woman. Can you say the same?

No, you can't since she walked in on you with someone that doesn't even compare to her. You're naïve as hell. It's a wrap for you," LeBron told Kayson.

"You better back the fuck down, boy. If my brother said that Toccara was his bitch, then she's his bitch. You can take your broken-ankle, needle-neck, Barney–built ass on somewhere before you get your ass beat in here," I warned LeBron. I'd had enough of his mouth. Kayson knew that he messed up. He didn't need anyone to remind him or keep rubbing the shit in.

"Kayson. Kyson. What's going on?" Estelada came prancing inside the police station.

"We have to get our women out of jail. They in here for some shit about assault," Kayson explained.

"Did they do it?" Estelada asked.

"We need to go somewhere private and talk," Kayson told her. He did correct by asking for privacy. There were too many eyes and ears around us, including LeBron's turkey-neck ass.

"It's okay. I already know what's up. Let me go see what I can find out. We need to see if we can get them on the docket today to see the judge. If not, they are going to have to stay the night," she told us.

"The hell you preach. I got Mone't pregnant earlier today. Ain't no way in hell she's staying the night anywhere but in the bed with me," I told her.

"We didn't need to hear that," Kayson blurted out.

"Then close your ears, nigga. I said that to say that Mone't's ass was going to be home tonight. You might as well go handle that shit," I ordered Estelada. She rolled her eyes and walked off. All we could hear were her heels clanking against the floor as she sashayed away.

"You need to be nicer to her. If not, she's going to stop fucking with us," Kayson fussed.

"A'ight. Damn. She better get my girl out, though," I grunted. Kayson shook his head.

"Let's go sit outside and wait. Being in here is causing me

anxiety. That shit with the cop pulling the gun on me still bothers me," Kayson admitted.

"I feel ya," I replied. "Aye, you need to be gone by the time we get back," I told LeBron. He glanced up at me from looking at his phone. I waited for him to say something, but he was smart enough to keep his mouth shut. He put his head back down and went back to focusing on whatever he had been doing with his phone.

Kayson and I walked outside to await news from Estelada. He was pacing back and forth enough to wear a hole in the concrete. He was a nervous wreck, and I hated that for him.

"Calm down, bro. It's going to be alright," I tried to assure him.

"It's not alright. I really liked Toccara, and I messed it up for some stale pussy. The shit crazy because I'm smarter than that. What would pops say about this?"

"Pops not the one you need to be worried about. Grandpa Robert is," I stated as I pointed at him. He was headed straight our way. "Kayson, look," I directed him. That was when he finally lifted his head and followed my finger.

There was no telling why Grandpa Robert was there. The look on his face suggested this wasn't going to be pretty at all. The best part about it was that I was sure his ass was there for Kayson and not me. It felt good to not be the problem child for once. Or so I thought.

3

KAYSON

Grandpa Robert popping up out of the blue wasn't good for anybody. He wore this expression of anger and disappointment. I dreaded what he was going to say or do when he reached us.

"Maybe he won't show out because of where we are," I stated to Kyson.

"Yeah right. Look who you're talking about. Grandpa Robert wouldn't care if you were at a church. If he has something he wants to get off his chest, he's going to do it," Kyson reminded me.

"What the hell is going on? I got a call that there were police at my pharmacy. Never in all the time that I was over that pharmacy did anything like that happen. Who wants to tell me what's going on?" he asked and then looked over at Kyson.

"Why are you looking at me like that? What makes you think I had something to do with this?"

"Because you always have something to do with mess and drama."

"Fuck this! I'm going back inside the station. I'll let you know when I know something. You can deal with his ass," Kyson told me.

"Don't you ever disrespect me like that again. I was there for you each time you got into trouble. You're too old for that shit now, Kyson." Grandpa Robert was going off on Ky for no reason. Preparing to say something to him, Kyson turned around and stopped me.

"For years, you and Pops treated Kayson like he was better than me. That's why I always went hard to get shit on my own. I'm sick of it. You're not about to blame me for something that happened at the pharmacy. The pharmacy that I was given no parts of. That's all him, homie." Kyson turned and prepared to walk away again.

"Your hardheaded ass is going to get enough of all this foolishness you're always involved in. I'm sick of your shit, Kyson" Grandpa Robert concluded.

"I'm sick of your shit too, old man. You think you're so much better than me, but I know about all the trouble you got into when you were younger. The fact that you were charged for manslaughter and spent some time in jail. The fact that you can't keep your wrinkled-up dick to yourself. You're no better than me, so back the fuck down," Kyson snapped. My mouth dropped at his level of disrespect for our grandfather, but I didn't blame him one bit.

For years, Kyson had gone out of his way to make up for the trouble he'd gotten into when he was younger. There wasn't a single person on this earth that could say they never did anything that they regretted. He was young and still trying to learn his way. They should've understood that. If anything, with the things that Kyson said our grandfather had gotten into trouble for, he should be one of the most understanding people out there. I wondered where he got the information from when I'd never heard any of it before.

"What did you say to me?" Grandpa Robert asked. He had to be as shocked as I was to hear the things coming out of Kyson's mouth.

"You heard exactly what I said to you. You walk around here like you're all holier than thou when you need to be on somebody's front pew. You are not about to keep coming for me, old man. I'm tired of it. I understand that I fucked up in the past, but I'm a changed man. If you can't see that, then something is wrong with you," Kyson grumbled.

"He has changed, and he's right. None of this had anything to do with him. It was all my doing, and it really had nothing to do with the pharmacy. Some shit happened inside the pharmacy because of Bree's ass. She couldn't deal with being terminated," I called myself explaining to him.

"Terminated? She'd been there forever. Why would you terminate her?" he frantically asked. I already knew where his mind was headed. He felt like he was about to get into trouble for some shit he'd done in his past. He placed a lot of fault on Kyson, but I, too, knew of some things that he'd done wrong, even though I never spoke on them.

"She kept overstepping her boundaries. She should've been gone. She didn't like to work. She wasn't good for shit. I'm sure it didn't bother you as long as she was sucking your wrinkled dick, right?" Kyson rattled off, speaking for me. My grandfather clammed up. Kyson knew way more than I gave him credit for. I thought I was the only one that knew Bree had indulged in a few sexual activities with my grandfather at some point. Yet, it didn't seem as bad as Kyson was making it sound.

"How dare you speak to me like that? I can't believe this shit," Grandpa Robert grunted. He looked like he wanted to hit Kyson. It was a mess. If they were to get to fighting, I wouldn't know whose side to take because I loved them both. However, Kyson was my brother. My twin. If push came to shove, I was going to have his back, no matter what.

"Well, believe it. Like I said, I'm sick of your shit. I've put up with it for years. Enough is enough," Kyson concluded before looking at me. "How the hell could you even sleep with a bitch that your grandfather stuck his dick inside of?" Kyson chided as he stared at me. "You nasty as fuck, bro!" he added.

"All she did was suck his dick. That ain't got shit to do with me. He kept her around, so I knew her head game had to be topnotch. Hell, when she wanted to do it to me, I let her get down to it. Don't worry. I never kissed the bitch," I blurted out. It was what it was. It wasn't like I could change anything that happened. Therefore, it was no need for me to feel bad about it. A hoe was going to be a hoe, and that was definitely what Bree was.

"Kayson, I need to speak to the two of you," Estelada stuck her head out of the police station and told us.

"Guess that's my cue to walk away from the bullshit," Kyson grumbled, glancing back over his shoulder at our grandfather and walking away.

"I'll explain everything to you later. I promise," I told my grandfather as I left him standing there and walked inside the police station to join Estelada and Kyson.

Estelada led us down a long, somewhat-dark hallway. There was an eerie feeling that came over me as I remembered the night the officer violated my civil rights. I wanted desperately to find him and do something to him to make him feel the way he'd made me feel.

"In here," Estelada stated, removing me from my thoughts. She held her hand out to point toward an empty room. Inside the room, I could clearly see that it was an interrogation room. Why she had us in there, I didn't know.

"What are we doing in here? We ain't do shit," Kyson barked.

"Here's the deal... Bree is willing to drop charges against Mone't if Mone't will agree not to go after her for the leaked video," Estelada informed us.

"Are you out of your fuckin' mind? She ruined my girl's reputation. She needs to pay for that shit."

"I get that. But if Mone't wants to get out of here with a clean record, she may want to do this."

"Have you talked to her about it?" Kyson asked.

"They are about to bring her in here no—" Before she could finish her statement, the door swung open, and in walked Mone't. She was being carried in by two cops.

"Damn. What you do for them to need two escorts on your ass?" Kyson chuckled.

"I'm 'bout to fuck some shit up if they don't get me out of here. I didn't even do anything," Mone't hollered.

"Calm down and come here, baby," Kyson said and pulled her in to him. Her hands were still cuffed behind her back so there wasn't anything she could do to return his warm gesture of care and concern.

"How can I calm down? This is the worst shit that has ever happened to me. I was wronged, yet I'm the one sitting behind bars," she cried.

"If it makes you feel any better, Bree and Toccara are behind bars with you," I told her.

"Do what? What do you mean Toccara is behind bars?" she asked, shocked at what she'd heard.

"They came to the pharmacy and picked up Toccara and Bree," I stated. Mone't dropped her head. Tears continued to flow down her face. She was scared. I didn't blame her. Jail wasn't a place anybody wanted to be. It was sad that something that was supposed to be shared between her and Jared ended up being shared with all of Moss Point, and she was facing consequences due to it. "Mone't, I need you to pay attention to Estelada. She has a way of getting you out of jail where you won't have anything on your record," I continued.

"What do you mean?" she quizzed.

"I got it from here," Estelada told the officers. I wasn't sure what type of pull she had, but she was able to get them to leave Mone't in the room with us. I was sure they were right outside the door. It didn't matter. None of us were crazy enough to try anything.

Mone't glimpsed up at Kyson. He nodded his head, and she

slowly walked over to the empty chair that was in front of Estelada. Estelada wasted no time getting down to business.

"I'm going to be honest with you, this is where we stand right now. Bree is the reason that you and Toccara were arrested. She said that you attacked her about a week ago."

"Yeah, but that was because the bitch leaked a tape of me having sex. That wasn't her right to do. I ended up losing out on so much because of it. People started harassing me and my family over the shit. That wasn't right."

"I understand that. You are right. She was wrong for that. However, she is willing to drop the charges against you if you are willing to not move forward with getting her arrested for leaking the video," Estelada explained.

"In other words, you want me to let her get away with it?" Mone't jumped up out of her seat. She moved so quickly, her chair fell backward and made a loud thudding noise. Keys were rattling from the other side of the door as police officers rushed inside the room to see what was going on.

"It's okay," Estelada told them. She threw her hand up to hold them off.

"Sorry," Mone't apologized.

"I understand that you are upset. I promise you that I would be too. I'm just telling you that Bree is willing to drop charges if you are. That doesn't mean she'll get off free. We will still sue her ass for what she did."

"She's broke. How the hell can she afford to pay me for pain and suffering?" Mone't asked.

"Here's the thing with that... Mone't, if we sue and win, which I'm sure will happen, she will have to come up with a way to pay you. If she gets a new job, we can garnish her check. Kayson has her social security number from her work records. We can subpoena those to keep him from getting into trouble, and we can trace her wherever she goes. We can take whatever she owns. Trust me, there is a way to get her ass," Estelada emphasized.

"What do you think?" she asked Kyson.

The whole time the two of them talked, I stood off in a corner. It had me flabbergasted. They were focusing on Mone't, but not a word was mentioned about Toccara. If she was willing to do all of that for Mone't, what would she be willing to do to help Toccara be set free?

4
MONE'T

Stepping inside the interrogation room, I was shocked to see Kyson and Kayson in there with the attorney. It was good that they were there because it meant I wouldn't have to reach out to my parents to let them know what happened. I was thankful that Toccara's family was out of the house when the police came because we would never hear the end of it.

"Mone't, I don't want to sound selfish, but if you could drop the charges against Bree, it would help Toccara out a lot," Kayson announced.

"Shut up talking to me, Kayson. If you never would've been fuckin' with Bree and trying to get with Toccara at the same time, then we wouldn't be in this situation. Everything that is going wrong in our lives is because of you and Bree. If she was so good to you, then why would you pursue Toccara?" I snapped on his ass.

"It wasn't like that. I swear it wasn't," he tried to defend himself.

"Whatever. You ain't got to lie to kick it. I may fuck with Kyson, but know that I don't like you. I don't like you for Toccara, and I hope she decides to leave you alone when she gets out," I admitted. Those words came from a place of hurt and anger.

"I'm not about to argue with you, Mone't. Either you are going to drop the charges, or you're not," Kayson muttered to me.

"Kyson, what would you do if you were me?" I asked Kyson again.

"I'm going to be completely honest with you. Kayson is my brother, and if we were in this situation, I'd let go of my ego and do whatever I could to get us both of out this mess. Yeah, Bree was wrong for what she did, but she won't be completely getting away with it. You can sue her and take her for everything that she has. That'll make her think twice about crossing someone else like that," Kyson stated. He rubbed me the wrong way when he said let go of my ego. People thought it was okay for others to wrong you and you were supposed to let it go so easily. I wasn't that type of bitch, and if I did decide to let this shit go, I was still going to beat Bree's ass again. Probably every time I saw her ass.

"This has nothing to do with my ego but everything to do with me protecting myself. If you can promise me that I can sue her and she won't get away with this, then I won't press charges on her."

"I can assure you that I will do any- and everything that I can to make sure that you receive some type of justice for what Bree did." There was a brief moment of silence in the room before Estelada started speaking again. "I need to let you all know that this is for Mone't only. Bree hadn't said anything about Toccara. I think she's highly upset with the way that Toccara kicked her ass," Estelada stated as she began to giggle. She was the only one laughing because we were all wondering what was going to happen with Toccara. If anything, she was the one that needed to be released. She had come too far to end up with something on her record because of Bree and Kayson's dumb asses.

"When are we going to handle things with Toccara?" Kayson

hollered. He punched the wall. The officers neared him and were getting ready to place him in cuffs, but Estelada was able to calm him down. For a brief moment, it seemed like I saw tears in Kayson's eyes. That was the first time I saw him being vulnerable. Hell, it was the first time I'd seen any man being vulnerable. That let me know that he had some type of feelings for Toccara. Was I wrong for the way that I was judging him? Hell naw. This was still all his fault.

"Let's get everything handled with Mone't first, and then I can work on Toccara. Her case is a little more complicated because she actually tried to beat the po' child to sleep in front of the cops."

"Wait... Toccara got her again?"

"Yep. She dog walked Bree's ass," Kayson beamed. He appeared happy, which caught me off guard. He had been going hard for Bree's ass up until this point, so what had changed?

"Fine. Get me out of here. I want a clean record and to start the process for suing that bitch, and I'll be fine. Do I need to get money together to get Toccara out? She can't stay in here," I whined.

"No. I got it. It's my fault, so I'll make sure she's fine. You get out, and you and Kyson can leave. I'm not leaving until Toccara is free," Kayson assured me.

"I'm not leaving until she's free either, so I guess we'll be some sitting ducks until we hear something," I told him.

"Fine," he grunted.

"Fine," I sassed, making sure I got the last word.

"Okay. The officers are going to take you back to your cell now. Let me go get all of this sorted out, and you should be out of here within the next two hours."

The officers took me back to the holding cell where I searched to see if I could see Bree or Toccara. I spotted Bree, but Toccara was nowhere to be found.

"Where's my friend with your dog ass?" I asked Bree when I laid eyes on her.

"Your guess is as good as mine. She should be the one back here, not me."

"Are you out of your mind? Do you know what you've done? You ruined my life, and I had nothing to do with your beef with Toccara. Truth be told, she was innocent through all of this as well. Kayson led you on, not her. Why would you try to hurt someone that can't control a man? He's a grown ass man and is going to pick the woman that he feels is best for him. Sorry, boo, but that ain't you." That was probably wrong for me to say, but who cared? That bitch needed to hear the truth.

"Whatever. Kayson loves me. He has to be reminded. That's all." She was still delusional, and it was almost sad. If she wanted to continue to feel that way, then that was on her. There wasn't shit else I was going to say on the subject. All I wanted to do was get the hell out of there.

Moving away from her, I marched toward the closest bench I could find in hopes of taking a seat. It was dirty, and so was the drunken lady laying down on it. Lucky for me, I was slender, or there would've been no way my ass would've fit on that bench. I used my right hand to try to dust the seat off and rubbed my hand across the gown I was still wearing before pulling it as far down under my butt as it would go and taking a seat.

"Who told you that you could sit down?" the woman abruptly sat up and asked me. She was wearing a torn white T-shirt that was covered in vomit and some torn jeans. She couldn't be serious with herself.

"I told myself I could sit down," I replied, rolling my eyes. Clearly, she didn't know better, or else she would've done better. She needed to go ask Bree how deadly my hands were before she came messing with me.

"You can't tell yourself anything. I run this cell here," she voiced.

"You can run whatever you want to run except me. Find somebody to play with because I'm not it," I sternly spoke.

"Better go ask that bitch about me," I added, pointing over to Bree.

"Don't send nobody over here to ask me shit. I beat your ass, and don't you forget it," Bree lied.

"What? You did what?" I couldn't believe my ears. She was blatantly lying and trying to hype herself up in front of these people we didn't know. That caused me to jump up off the bench and migrate toward her. I needed her to show me again how she "beat my ass".

"Let's go, Rogers," one of the officers yelled.

"This ain't over hoe," I told Bree as I made my way over to the cell door. I tapped my foot on the floor as I patiently waited for them to open it.

"Hey! What about me?" Bree yelled as soon as I stepped out of the cell.

The man closed the door back and looked at her before saying, "What about you?"

"I'm supposed to be let go too. What's going on?" she quizzed.

"You have charges against you by someone else."

"That's my bitch!" I exclaimed. It was no secret that Toccara wasn't going to let Bree off so easily.

Bree walked over to a corner in the cell and cowered down like a lost puppy. I stuck my tongue out at her and made a complete circle in the middle of the floor trying to see if I could locate Toccara anywhere. Not seeing her, I began to worry. Maybe they'd taken her to another jail. *Did she have to go before the judge? What the hell was going on?* All kinds of thoughts clouded my mind.

"Let's go unless you plan on staying here," the officer scolded. That was when I picked up my pace and walked right out behind him. My mind raced wondering where Toccara was. It didn't make sense that she was nowhere to be found when the guys said that she was arrested too.

It didn't take long for them to release me. I didn't have any belongings, so there was nothing for me to sign for. I immediately ran into Kyson's awaiting arms when I saw him. Wrapping my arms around his neck, I closed my eyes and gently exhaled. As we were walking out the door, I noticed Estelada standing in front of a desk speaking to someone. I was hopeful that the conversation was about Toccara and she could tell me what was going on with her.

Taking it upon myself, I stopped and tapped her on the shoulder. I opened my mouth to speak, but my words immediately became caught in my throat when I saw Toccara walking past me. She was walking hand in hand with LeBron. Neither of us said a word. She glanced over at me and winked. I smirked and winked back as they continued on out the door. Something had to have gone down with Kayson for her to be with LeBron because we all knew that she didn't want his ass. Kayson stood there like a bump on a log. Not once did he open his mouth and say anything, and that to me was a punk ass move. If he wanted Toccara the way he claimed, he would've been fighting for her. She had just pulled the biggest checkmate card of the year, and I wasn't mad at all.

5
TOCCARA

Surprisingly, when I got to the jail, I never saw the back. They took me to the room for booking but immediately stopped and had me follow one of the officers to an interrogation room where an attorney was sitting and waiting for me. I was expecting to see Estelada only because deep down inside, I wanted Kayson to come through for me. He at least owed me that much. Instead, there was this heavy-set, short Caucasian man. He wore his spectacles on the bridge of his nose. He reminded me so much of Joe Pesci with his George Jefferson haircut.

"Have a seat, Ms. Jones," he told me. "I'm Attorney Grisby, and I was hired by LeBron to represent you. I need for you to tell me everything that happened from beginning to end. Be sure not to leave anything out," he told me. Very intently, he sat there and listened to every word that left my mouth. That was crazy considering I was never used to a man listening to me like that. It was like he was hanging on to my every word. "Are you saying that they never read you your rights?" he asked me.

"No. They didn't."

"Try to be sure. At no point of them being there did they tell you your rights from the time they stepped inside the pharmacy to the time you were arrested?" he asked for clarity.

"No. They just told me I was being arrested for assault because of Bree's bitch ass." A small smirk came across his face before he told me to sit tight, and he walked out the room. He returned almost thirty minutes later with LeBron. He told me that I would, hopefully, be free to go soon. I was confused because I didn't know what he was talking about and didn't believe him. Not wanting to be a fool and try to walk away, I remained seated at the table, refusing to move. I was too worried the police would think I was trying to escape and shoot me in the back or something. "Huh? What's going on?" I finally found the voice to speak.

"They didn't Mirandize you at any point, so nothing you said or did when they arrived can be used against you. I heard all about you fighting, but they can't use that against you. This is really an open and shut case," he explained.

"What about my record? Is it going to pop up that this happened? I'll never be able to get a job or get into another residency program again." I began to cry.

"If there are no charges pressed against you and you are not found guilt, then none of this will be on your record. You did nothing wrong. You were protecting yourself like any other human being would do," he expressed. That sounded good to me.

"Wait... What about the original reason the police came looking for me? She had to have told them that I jumped on her before," I acknowledged.

"Actually, I heard about the situation with the video she leaked. She mentioned your name but placed most of the blame on your friend, Mone't. At this point, I'm going to see if I can use the fact that you weren't Mirandized to at least get you released. We can deal with her original problem later," he told me. The things he said sounded good, but for some reason, I didn't trust him. Shit, look who hired him. I damn sure didn't trust LeBron. In my opinion, anybody working with his ass had to be a snake too. Right now, it didn't matter. All I wanted to do was go home and reevaluate my life.

LeBron and I sat in the interrogation room waiting for Attorney Grisby to return. When he did, he told me that I could go. I took LeBron's hand because I knew I was going to end up walking past Kayson at some point. He needed to see that what he didn't value another man did. No sooner than we rounded the corner, I ran straight into him, Kyson, and Mone't. Winking at Mone't, I kept walking out the door. I'd have to let her in on what was going on with me later. It wasn't the time then, because I wanted Kayson to feel the same hurt I felt when I saw him with Bree's retarded ass.

Attorney Grisby and LeBron spent a few more minutes talking as we made our way toward his car. I leaned against the car as the two of them continued to talk. It took some time for LeBron to think about me standing out there before he finally unlocked the door. Quickly, I slid inside the car. I'd already faced enough embarrassment for today. I didn't want anybody else passing by and seeing me standing outside of the police station for them to start calling and trying to find out why I was out there. I certainly didn't need them calling my parents to see what was going on with me.

LeBron finally joined me inside the car. He made sure to slam the door, causing me to be removed from my thoughts.

"You good? You ready to go? You hungry, baby?" he asked me.

"Yes, I'm good. Yes, I'm ready to go. No, I'm not hungry. Can you just take me to get my car so I can go home?" I responded to him, not trying to hide the fact that I was annoyed.

"Don't be catching an attitude with me. All I'm trying to do is make sure you're okay. Remember who was there for you to help get you out," he boasted.

"You happy that you had to lie? What was so special about that? Lying is like a second job for your ass, or did you forget how you kept your wife and kids from me?" I reminded him.

"Stop bringing up things that are irrelevant to what we got going on now. I'm trying to make all of this better."

"There's nothing you can do to make any of this better but take me to my car so I can go home. That's the only thing I want you to do for me right now or ever again."

"I'm not taking you to your car. I'm going to take you home, so I'll know that you got there safely."

"I'm not a child. I know how to drive myself home."

"You were acting like one earlier with all that damn fighting, so keep that same energy. I told you that I was driving you home, and that's that. No need for you to do all of that talking back because I don't want to hear that shit."

There was a time that I would've argued with him, but I didn't feel like it today. If he wanted to take me home, that was fine. Mone't was out, so she could always take me to get my car later. Or I could get my sister Olivia to take me.

"What are you plotting?" LeBron asked after a long moment of silence.

"What? What are you talking about?" I quizzed. He was getting weirder by the minute. I couldn't wait for him to drop me off.

"You're quiet. It's never good when you're quiet," he acknowledged.

"I have a lot on my mind. Leave me alone," I snapped, sick of his shit.

The remainder of the ride was done in complete silence. Arriving at my house, I didn't wait for him to put the car in park before I jumped out and went straight to my door. It dawned on me when I got there that my keys were inside my purse at the pharmacy. I didn't even have my cell phone on me. Luckily, I kept a spare on the top of the doorframe. I surveyed the scene to make sure nobody was watching before I stood on my tiptoes to retrieve the key. I rushed to open the door, but it was no use because by then, LeBron had gotten out of the car and was on my heels.

"I'm home. You may leave," I told him as I attempted to shut the door on him. He stuck his foot inside the door, preventing me from shutting it. "What are you doing?" I probed.

"I want to talk to you about a decision that I made. Let me come in for a minute," he commented, licking his crusty ass lips.

"No. I'm tired and want to relax. We can talk some other time," I told him.

"I'm not stupid, Toccara. You're going to tell me that we can talk later, and all you're going to do is dodge my fuckin' calls. Quit playing with me," he ordered.

"Who's playing with you? I said I don't want to talk. Back the fuck down," I barked, getting in his face.

"Girl, you better get your short ass out of my face. I don't hit women, but I swear I have no problem getting my sister to beat your ass," he insisted.

"She can try, but I promise it won't work out the way you think it will. Besides, why you got to get your sister? You got a whole wife. I'm sure she would love to fight me."

"That's what I want to talk to you about." LeBron suddenly put his hand on my chest and forcefully pushed me out of the way. He walked around me and headed straight for my couch. He took a seat without me inviting him to do so.

"You need to leave," I demanded.

"I need to, but I'm not. You might as well sit down and talk to me because I'm not leaving until you hear me out." *Who was he to come in my home and make demands?* He was acting mad at me when he was the one that wronged me. What kinda shit was that?

"Leave, LeBron. I'm not playing with you. Get out of my house," I hollered. He glimpsed over at me and proceeded to turn his attention back to my coffee table. He picked the remote up and flicked the TV on as if I didn't say anything to him. It was pissing me off more and more. I stormed out of the living room and went inside my bedroom.

Inside my nightstand was a spare taser that I kept in there

for niggas like him. I grabbed it out and went right back inside my living room area. Not saying a word to him, I turned the taser on and stuck my hand out preparing to stick his ass. He had to have seen my reflection through the TV because he leaned to the side causing me to lose my balance and fall onto the couch. The taser fell out of my hand as LeBron caught me and kept me from bouncing off the couch and onto the floor.

"Stop acting this way with me, Toccara. I'm trying to fix the shit that I did to you. I know you heard me talking to the attorney. I filed for a divorce, baby. I want to be with you and only you," he stared into my eyes and announced.

"That's cool that you want to be with me, but I don't want to be with you. You had me and didn't do right by me, and I'm not giving you the chance to hurt me like that ever again. You took a vow before God with that woman and continuously cheated on her. If you'd cheat on her, then I know you'd cheat on me. Now, like I said, get up and get out," I sassed as I placed my palms down on the couch to hold my balance and push myself up off the couch. LeBron wasn't letting go. He wrapped his arms around me tighter.

"I'm never letting you go, Toccara. I don't care how mad you get. I'm not. We are meant to be," he argued with me.

"Boy, bye! Get lost," I hollered, yet he still wouldn't let me go.

Click... Click...

Frozen in my tracks, I wouldn't move when I heard the clicking of a gun. LeBron heard it too because he let me go. I continued on with my initial plan of getting off the couch and out of his reach. On my feet, I was stunned when I saw Kayson standing there with a gun in his hand.

"She's not going to have to tell you again to get the fuck out, is she?" he asked LeBron.

LeBron was such a scary ass. He stood from the couch and held his hands up in the air. He shook his head and began moving toward the door. I shook my head at how much of a coward he'd turned into. All he had to do was leave in the first place, and none of this would be happening.

"What are you doing here?" I asked Kayson while LeBron marched toward the door.

"I'm not him. We weren't together when I fucked Bree, so I wasn't cheating on you. I'd never cheat on you. The reason I didn't say shit at the pharmacy was because I was disappointed in myself and didn't know what to say. I'm sorry, Toccara. You told me to come to you when I was ready to let Bree go, and I'm ready, baby," he pleaded with me.

"I want you to go. I don't want either of you to be here. I don't care about you being ready now. You should've been ready when I first said something to you about it. If you wanted me, you never would've let me leave that night. You should've made it known to her that what you had with her was over and you should've left it at that. Nobody can force you into anything you don't want to do. If you think you're going to hit me with that shit again about how she was just there and you weren't thinking straight, then guess again. I don't want to hear it. You did what you did and showed me your true colors. Now, get the fuck out of here. I'll pick up my shit and last paycheck by Friday." I threw up my middle finger and stuck my tongue out at him. Was it childish? I didn't give a damn. He and LeBron both needed to get the fuck out of my face.

Kayson was hesitant, but he eventually went out the door behind LeBron. It wasn't shit either of them could say to me to change the way that I felt. They both failed me.

6

KYSON

One Week Later...

After all the shit that happened with Mone't, Toccara, and Bree, I had Mone't staying at a hotel. She and Toccara were best friends, but I felt they needed to be separated for a while until we could get things cleared up. There was also still the issue about the video. It had died down some, but people knew where Toccara lived and went by there looking to harass them both. Mone't came with me willingly. Kayson was still trying to shoot his shot with Toccara, but she wasn't playing with his ass when she said that she was done with him. Bree's ass was still in jail, as far as we knew, because that LeBron nigga kept up the lie about her hitting him or whatever he said to the cops. She couldn't afford an attorney, and the public defender she was assigned wasn't really fuckin' with her. If you had any involvement with the law whether it was you, a family member or friend, then you would understand what I meant about the issue with the public defender.

"Kyson, I'm sick of being in this hotel," Mone't whined, jumping from under the covers. She was naked as the day she was born. I licked my lips because I wanted her lil' ass so bad.

However, I had to show her that I understood how she felt, first. Sexing her was going to have to wait.

She told me that being at the hotel was lonely for her unless, I stopped by, she went to see Toccara, or she visited her parents. I understood that.

Mone't still managed to keep the incident with her going to jail away from her parents. As far as they knew, she was still staying at a hotel to hide from the people harassing her behind the video. I tried to spend as much time with her as I could, but that wasn't as much as I wanted because I had the kids at home. The one positive thing about all of this was that Mone't never complained about where I was spending my time because she knew that if I wasn't working, I was either going to be with her, or I was going to be with the kids.

"I know, and I understand. How do you feel about coming to the house this weekend?" I asked her.

"The kids must be going on vacation or something?" she inquired. I laughed because of the goofy look she had plastered all over her face.

"No. They are going to be at home. Why would I make them go somewhere for you to come over?"

"So you're saying you want me to meet the kids?" she asked, seeming confused.

"Yes, Mone't. I know we haven't been together long, but it's been long enough. I really like you, and if you're going to be in my life, you will be in their lives too. I need to make sure you can build a relationship with them," I explained.

"What you mean? Them not even your kids," she blurted out, causing me to cringe. I hated when people told me that. Even though I didn't take part in their creation, they have always been more of mine then they were Cyn's.

"Mone't, I like you, but I will leave your ass alone if I hear you say that stupid shit again. No, I didn't nut in the bitch to make them, but those are my kids. If you still on that not wanting to be a step-momma bullshit, tell me now. I have no problem leaving."

"Wow. You going to walk away from me that easily?"

"Hell yeah. I'd never put a woman or anyone else before my kids."

"Fine. If it means that much to you, I'll meet the kids. I don't want any shit behind it either, Kyson."

"What you mean?" I quizzed, wondering what she was talking about.

"You better not have those kids terrorize me to see what I can put up with. I'm not playing with you." She carried a serious expression on her face. I laughed so hard I had to grab my stomach. That would've been funny as hell. She didn't have to worry about me getting them to terrorize her. That was something they'd do on their own if they didn't like her.

Some people might think it was too soon for Mone't to meet the kids, but I'd been knowing her for two months. At least that was when I laid eyes on her—two months ago. Since that day, she'd been on my mind. That had never happened to me before. The fight she put up, the snapper between her legs, and that smart-ass mouth was something I wasn't prepared to let go of any time soon. Nor was I going to let the kids go. Plus, I wanted to get her out of the hotel and in the house with me. I wanted to be able to wrap my arms around her every night. Close my eyes next to her. Wake up to her wolf breath in the mornings. That couldn't happen until she met the kids and I saw that she knew how to be around them, how to deal with them, and was capable of loving them as much as I did. It would take some time for the love to develop, but I was prepared for it.

"You laughing and I'm serious. Don't play with me, Ky. I'll fuck you and them lil' boogers up. I fight kids too," she exclaimed. The look in her eyes told me that her ass was serious. The way she fucked Bree up, I wasn't willing to risk her fucking up one of the kids.

"I can see you now down on your knees trying to box one of my babies out," I said and laughed even harder.

"I hate you," she stated. She called herself putting her arms across her chest and pouting. That didn't last long. The more I laughed, the harder it became for her to hold her laughter in. I grabbed her by the waist and pulled her in close to me.

"I'd never put you in a bad situation," I stopped laughing long enough to tell her.

"I hope not because if you do that shit your brother did to my girl, I'm going to be on the ten o'clock news," she assured me, never cracking a smile.

"I hear ya. Now lay down. I'm trying to spread your legs like butter," I stated. It was hard for me to continue to be serious with her when she was standing next to me naked.

"You so damn nasty. I love it." She giggled.

Mone't lifted my left hand up to her mouth and stuck two of my fingers inside of it. She began seductively sucking on them while placing her right hand on my chest and allowing it to roam down my body. When she reached my pants, she undid my belt and unbuttoned my pants, allowing them to drop down to my ankles. She kept my fingers in her mouth as she slowly dropped down to her knees. She removed my fingers from her mouth and placed her mouth on the top of my boxers. She bit into them and used her teeth to pull them down. The shit was sexy as hell. Mone't was going out of her way to please me. That didn't happen too often. I was used to bitches giving me basic head and letting me fuck them in every hole they had. That was their way of letting me please them. There was no way any other woman would be able to please me the way Mone't did. That was another reason I wasn't trying to let her go.

"Damn, ma," I muttered when she got my boxers down and began licking on my dick.

Anticipating her pulling my mans into her mouth, she did the complete opposite. She spit on my dick and used her hands to massage it as she turned her head sideways and started dipping my balls in and out of her mouth. My knees became weak. It felt like I was about to fall. I needed to get to the bed or wall before she had me crying in this muthafucka like a lil' bitch.

"Chill out, Mone't," I grunted.

"Naw. You wanna spread these legs, you gotta work for it. Take this shit like a man," she stated. That was where she fucked up. I couldn't keep standing there like a mannequin from Old Navy. Mone't was about to get this work.

"Open your mouth," I ordered, glaring into her eyes. She had a worried expression on her face, but she never said a word.

As soon as she opened her mouth, I plunged my dick deep down her throat. She instantly began gagging. That didn't stop me. She wanted to be nasty, so I was going to help her out. I pushed a little deeper inside her throat and placed my hand on the back of her head to keep her from moving. She remained on her knees with slobber running down the sides of her mouth and tears dropping from her eyes.

"You like that shit, don't you? I'm giving you that work now, huh?" I boasted, removing my dick long enough for her to answer.

"Fuck you, Kyson," she blurted out with a smirk on her face before engulfing my dick in her mouth all over again. My eyes immediately rolled to the back of my head as she began to deep throat my shit. She was pulling my dick in and out of her mouth, even deeper than I had pushed it in before. Mone't was moaning and shit. The vibrations from her moans were about to drive me crazy. Mone't was about to catch these throat babies before she felt me inside of her if she kept that shit up.

"Shit," I grunted. "You trynna make a nigga bust."

Mone't moved her head back and forth on my dick, coating my dick with all her saliva. I closed my eyes and imagined being inside of her as she clamped her lips down as tight as she could. It felt almost as tight as I remembered her pussy feeling the night before. My nut was building more and more. The moment she cuffed my balls to massage them, I could no longer take it. I snatched my dick out of her mouth, leaned down to pick her up, flipped her upside down, and stuck my head in her pussy. In that moment, Mone't was like Baskin-Robbins. I wanted all of her thirty-one flavors.

"Suck yo' dick, ma," I instructed her.

"I can't. You're eating your pussy too good," she moaned. A smile crept upon my face.

Dipping my tongue in and out of her juicy, wet pussy, I felt her juices running out. She was trembling in my arms, so I gripped her tighter to make sure she wouldn't fall. To add to the pleasure I was giving her, I stuck a finger inside of her pussy. Wiggling it around, I got it wet enough to slide inside her ass. She tensed up when she felt me attempt to push my finger in. She clamped her ass cheeks and legs together. She was damn near crushing my head.

Pop... Pop...

Removing my right hand to pop her on the ass, I stopped eating her pussy long enough for her to unclamp her shit.

"Don't fight me, ma," I told her.

"I'm not ready to cum," she squealed.

"Don't worry. It's not going to be the only nut you get," I told her as I sucked my finger and slithered it right inside of her ass. She tried to break free from me, but nothing she did worked. I placed my mouth right back on her pussy and began slurping and sucking on it. Mone't started hollering like someone was killing her. That made me go harder with what I was doing to her. I picked up my pace with finger fucking her in the ass and licking on her pussy until she couldn't take it anymore. The minute she began shaking and squirting, I removed my finger from her ass and placed both of my arms around her to keep from dropping her.

"Ssssshhhhhh..."

"Let that shit go, ma."

Placing my mouth back on her pussy, I tried to catch as much of her juices as I could. Mone't tasted good as fuck. I didn't want to take her pussy out of my mouth ever, but my dick wanted some attention. We moved over to the bed, and I gently laid her down. Her body was limp. That nut had taken a lot out of her. That was fine because I was about to give her ass a second burst of energy.

Climbing in the bed with her, I weaseled my body between her legs. My dick was already hard, but it wasn't as hard as I wanted it to be. That was when I used it to massage her clit.

"I can't take anymore," she whined.

"Shut up with that shit. You 'bout to get all this dick," I told her, and meant every word.

Mone't glanced up at me with lust in her eyes. That caused me to lick my lips again. We locked eyes as I slowly slid inside of her. Mone't's body bucked a little. As much as I'd been inside of her, she should've been used to my size. However, I noticed that she always tensed up immediately after I entered her. As usual, I allowed her to move her body around a little to get comfortable with me being inside of her.

"Fuck. You need to get a smaller dick," she spoke.

"Naw. You need to get used to taking this dick. Another nigga can't even sniff your mufuckin' pussy. You hear me?" I commented.

"Yes, Kyson," she replied, rolling her eyes.

Pop...

Without warning, I popped her on the thigh.

"What the fuck?" She gasped.

"Put some mufuckin' respeck on my name. You know what the fuck it is. Say it the right way and without all that fuckin' attitude," I ordered before pushing deeper inside of her.

"Fuckkkkkkk..." she moaned.

"Say my name."

"Kyson!"

Pop...

"Don't fuckin' play with me, Mone't. You know what the fuck I want to hear."

"Kyson!"

Pop...

The longer she played with me, the more I popped her and the deeper I pushed inside of her.

"Shiittttt... You're fuckin' me too good. You're gonna make me cum again," she announced.

"Say my muthafuckin' name, Mone't," I ordered once more.

"I'm cummin', Kyson. Fuckkkkkkk..." she exclaimed. That made me pull out of her. She had me fucked up if she thought she was 'bout to get another nut without me getting what I wanted out of her. "No, baby. Don't do me like that," she cried.

"Naw. You need to do what the fuck I said do. Fuck around and get put on dick punishment. You know you don't want that with your freaky ass," I told her.

"Put it back in. Please, baby. Don't do that," she continued to whine. "I'll do whatever you say," she finally stated with pleading eyes.

Gradually, I pushed back inside of her. Her body lifted off the bed a bit. Mone't was so wet I thought I was about to bust without having a chance to pump inside of her a few more times. She knew that it felt good. She became petty and squeezed her pussy muscles around my dick as hard as she could before pushing up and grinding on me.

"This shit is mine, forever," I announced. I'd never told a female that a day in my life. Mone't needed to know that me saying that to her was because I meant it, and I'd fuck up her and anyone else that I had to behind the shit.

"Forever? You sure you want this forever?" she sensually commented.

"You heard what the fuck I sa—"

There was never a chance for me to finish my statement. When I thought Mone't couldn't squeeze any tighter, she fucked me up by squeezing my shit like her pussy was a pair of vice grips. I damn near lost my mind. Badly, I wanted to tell her to loosen her grip, but the way it felt, I couldn't. Mone't had the type of pussy that would have a nigga wanting to repent when it was all said and done.

"You like that shit, my big dick monster?" she quizzed, smiling. That was all I wanted to hear her say.

Not being the one to ever back down or tap out, I bit down on Mone't's left breast. That caused her to release the hold she had on my dick. Gaining a second wind, I stroked in and out of her as if I'd never get the chance to feel her again. Pushing her legs up until they were damn near behind her head, I picked my body up and sent my dick slamming back inside of her. Mone't hollered out and began erratically clawing at my back. That was exactly what I wanted her to do. All that shit she thought she was doing by squeezing my mans, but she needed to know who was in charge.

"What's my muthafuckin' name?" I asked in the middle of sliding in and out of her.

"Big dick monster! Shiiiiaaaattttt... I'm cummin'," she announced.

Uncontrollable shakes. Trembles. Heavy breathing. Constant clawing at my back. Squeezing her pussy muscles. Finally, squirting. Mone't couldn't control herself. The moment I felt her juices coming out, I pulled out of her and allowed her to release on the bed. Putting my face between her legs, I did my best to catch as much of her tasty nectar as I could. It seemed like she'd been squirting for damn near an hour when it was probably no longer than a few seconds. Her body went limp on the bed, but I wasn't done with her. I moved back up and slid back inside of her.

"I can't take anymore," she exclaimed once again, tapping out on me.

"Naw. You got this, ma. We in this shit together. Ain't no one person nuttin' and the next person ain't. I'm not with that shit," I grunted, continuously gliding in and out of her. She wrapped her arms around my neck and held on for dear life. Instead of being rough with her, I took my time. I leisurely entered her and would pull all the way back out. Several times of doing so, I laid off in it and wiggled my dick around, grinding inside of her.

"Mmmm... You're gonna make me cum again," she told me.

"Let that shit go, ma," I ordered. That was because I was finally about to nut too.

Before I had a chance to release, I heard her say, "Shit, Ky. Here it comes." Once she'd made her little announcement, she began shaking again. This time, she didn't squirt, but I felt her creaming all over my dick, making it slippery. That helped me to grind better inside of her. It wasn't a good two minutes after she'd finished that I'd finally allowed my seeds to seep out inside of her.

My body was drained. There was barely enough air inside of me for me to control my breathing. Before I could get up to move to the side of her and hold her, Mone't jerked me down on top of her. My head lay on her chest as she played in my hair. My dick was still semi-erect inside of her.

"You know you just got me pregnant, right?" Mone't stated out of nowhere. Hearing that didn't make me mad. It didn't make me want to move or regret what I'd done. Hell, I thought I'd gotten her pregnant the day she was arrested. If it didn't happen that day, it sure as hell had to have happened this time.

Had she been anyone else, I would've jumped out of the bed like a flash of lightening and made her go clean herself up, drink vinegar or some shit, and take that morning-after pill. Since it was Mone't, I was filled with excitement on the inside. She knew her body better than anyone else, and if she felt like I'd just given her a blessing, I was all for it.

So, instead of making it an awkward moment, I simply replied, "I know, baby. I know."

7

MONE'T

The sex session that Kyson and I had was everything to me. It was like we started out straight fuckin', but it turned into a lovemaking session. It was weird because the way I felt for him was nowhere near the way I once felt about Jared, and it worried me. *Could I have fallen for Kyson already?* It was a weird feeling, yet it was great at the same time. He was making me feel the way I'd always wanted a man to make me feel.

The fact that he told me that he wanted me to meet the kids caught me off guard. It didn't seem to me that we were at that point in our relationship. However, I wasn't going to fight him on it. I'd already made him mad when I rejected him the moment I found out about the kids. If I would've told him no, he might've thought that I didn't want anything to do with them, but that was far from the truth. Was I scared to meet them? Of course. I was the baby in my family. None of my friends or family members had babies or young kids. Hell, I probably didn't know how to hold a baby without dropping it. Shit, I was more concerned with feeling the dick than what the dick could produce. So, kids were the last thing on my mind. Now that I had no choice but to face the fact that they do exist in his world, it was going to be something that I had to deal with because Kyson wasn't about to walk out of my life. If he tried, I was cutting that nigga's feet off. He had used his dick to baptize my pussy and soul. That meant, like God, he was going to have to be my protector and provider forever.

My ignorant ass started giggling at my thoughts as I stood in the shower washing all the sex and sweat off me.

"Fuck you laughing at, weird ass?" Kyson stormed inside the bathroom and asked. He was still naked, so I assumed he was ready for me to get out so he could get in. I suggested that we shower together, but he told me no because I'd be touching him, and we'd be back to where we started. He had to go check on the kids, so he couldn't even give me a quickie. I didn't complain, because like I told him earlier, I didn't have any more in me. My pussy was swollen and needed a break from his ass. Shit, he could stay gone for a few days if he wanted. My "good girl" needed to recuperate.

"I was thinking about something. Why are you coming in here without knocking?" I asked him, trying to seem like I had an attitude.

"Do I knock on your pussy before I cum inside of it?"

"Actually, you beat the fuckin' walls down. Don't play with me, Kyson. Your mouth always gotta be so smart."

"You right. My thang be thangin', huh?" he boasted, hitting himself in the chest like he was Tarzan. I couldn't help but laugh at how goofy his ass was. Kyson had a smart-ass mouth true enough. At the same time, he was silly. We stayed laughing at something, and I loved it. Finding a man like him had definitely been hard for me. "Hurry up, bae. I want to go take the kids to get something to eat."

"Huh? I thought you were spending the day with me."

"I am. With you and the kids. Now let's go. My pops called and said I needed to get home anyways."

"Then get in with me and we'll be done in no time," I instructed him.

"Hell naw. You can't keep your hands to yourself," he told me.

"Shut up. That be your mannish ass. Now come on," I ordered. He shook his head but hurried and got in the shower with me. We took turns cleaning each other off before I got out. I'd already basically finished showering before he got in anyways. Me getting out was giving him a little more time to make sure he was as clean as he wanted to be.

Wrapping the towel around me, I brushed my teeth and went inside the room to pull something to wear out of the dresser. It was warm outside, so I decided on a camouflage romper that was sleeveless. I had some wedges that were the same dark-green color in my romper that I knew would set it off perfectly. I continued to get dressed while Kyson was still in the bathroom. By the time he walked out, I was finishing up with moisturizing my body so I could go in the bathroom and do something to my messy ass hair. Leave it to Kyson to sweat my shit out so bad that I looked like a damn rag doll.

"What are you going to do about that wolf hair on your head?" he asked as he marched inside the room with a towel wrapped around his body. He wasn't completely dry, so the tiny droplets of water that were still on him radiated with a touch of the lighting in the room. Without hesitation, I licked my lips. My man was fine as fuck. The more I looked at him, the more I wondered why I was ever with Jared's ass in the first place. Kyson was gorgeous and had the dick to match. Jared looked okay but he was overly cocky, and his dick looked like black licorice. Love had me blinded by his ass. It'd never happen again. "Aye, chill out with licking your lips and shit. You not getting no more dick for a while. You trying to break my shit off," he joked.

"Not unless I'm breaking it off inside of me," I cooed, winking at him.

"Mannnn... Fuck all that."

Kyson marched over toward me. He picked me up and carried me over to where the TV stand was. Without saying anything, he placed me back on my feet, turned me to face the

TV, kicked my legs apart like he was a cop engaging in a search, and pulled my romper and thong to the side. Kyson entered me without a problem because I was already super wet from looking at him.

"You gonna quit playing with a nigga, ain't ya?"

"Yes, baby. I'm not going to do that shit no more." I didn't know what the fuck he was talking about that I did, but I went with the flow because the feelings he was giving me were too real.

"Throw that ass back," he demanded.

Pop... Pop...

Kyson had the nerve to pop me on the ass. That shit stung. My body bucked after each lick. I gripped the TV stand and began throwing my ass back as he requested. I was literally standing there twerking on his dick. The sound of him grunting turned me on. He wanted to give me a quickie, and I was going to show him how quick it could be. Moving my romper over a little more before spitting on my hand and rubbing it on my ass. I leaned up enough to make his dick fall out of me. Swiftly, I grabbed it and stroked it a few times before using my hand. I attempted to guide him inside of my ass. It had been a while since I allowed anyone to enter that domain, but I wanted to try it with Kyson.

"Naw, ma. Not like this," he quipped and pulled back. "If we take it there, it's going to hurt, and you're going to bleed. I don't need you walking around like you just got off a horse when you meet the kids. Plus, shit like that takes time and patience. I'll feel all of your holes soon enough," he explained and re-entered my wet and awaiting pussy.

I was beyond speechless at the way he stopped me. Any other man would've dove right on in without giving it a second thought. The way that he cared meant a lot. Although I wanted to feel him in my ass, I understood where he was coming from. There was always a time and place to do certain things. Since it would be our first time doing anal together, I could understand wanting it to be done right.

"We'll finish this later," Kyson stated as he pulled out of me again. I wanted to fight his ass. How the hell he get started making me feel good and then stop so abruptly?

"What are you doing?" I asked.

"Chill yo' fast ass out. I'm going to handle all that later. My pops calling me, so something gotta be going down. Clean yo'self up and let's roll," he said. He went inside the bathroom and cleaned himself up before coming out and putting his clothes back on.

Stepping inside the bathroom, I removed my clothes and cleaned myself in the sink before changing my thong and putting my romper back on. I threw my hair in a messy bun, and we headed out of the room and straight to his car.

"What exactly are we doing today?" I probed. It was too silent in the car, and it was making me nervous. I was willing to take whatever conversation I could get at this point.

"Take the kids to eat and probably to the park or something," he simply replied. His demeanor had changed, and it started to worry me.

"What's wrong?"

"Why you asking so many questions?" He called himself chuckling to take away from the fact that his ass was being extremely rude.

"Either answer the question nicely, or don't say shit at all. Rude ass," I snapped on him. I knew how his mouth was, but I preferred the sweet Kyson over the bullshitter he was acting like at the moment.

"My bad, Mone't. Apparently, a letter came in the mail for me today and my pops said it's extremely urgent. I'm trying to get there to see what it's about. Things have been great for me right now with the kids, my relationship with my pops, and work." He stopped talking. My eyebrows furrowed when he didn't mention me.

"Ahem..." I cleared my throat.

"What? You still got my seeds stuck in your throat?"

"Don't play with me, Kyson." I playfully punched him in the shoulder.

"Mone't, you trippin'. You know you are definitely one of the best things that's happened to me in a long time. I may not act like it at times, but please understand that I appreciate you being in my life and the things you've done for me. The way you make me feel is unreal at times. I enjoy being around you."

"Awwww... Let me find out you crushin' on ya girl."

"Crushin'? Girl, please. I done hit that too many times for it to be a mufuckin' crush. I'm runnin' shit 'round here. I'm King Ding-A-Ling," he boasted.

"Shittin' me. The way I be having you screaming. Boy, you're more like King Scream-A-Lot," I jokingly replied.

"Fuck you, Mone't. Always crushin' a nigga's hopes and dreams," he stated. We both fell out laughing.

Kyson and I continued to laugh and joke all the way to his house. It was the first time since we'd been a couple that I'd actually been to his home. It was nice. He got out of the car first and then came and opened my door like the perfect gentleman. It was extremely sweet, and I loved it. If he continued to keep that up, he was going to get a nice treat later.

"Come on, baby." He held his hand out and assisted me with getting out of the car. I wasted no time hopping out and grabbing ahold of his arm. I wanted to stay as close to him as I could in case things didn't go as planned with the kids.

"Pops, where you at?" he called out to his father when we walked inside. That was the first time I thought about the fact that not only was I meeting his kids, but I was meeting his father. That was a big step for us. *Could he have really been serious when he said that he wanted me to be the woman in his life forever?* That was the only time someone allowed you to meet their parents, right? "Why you holding me so tight?" he asked, removing me from my thoughts.

"I'm excited. You are letting me meet your father. That's big, baby," I replied before standing on my tiptoes and placing a kiss on his cheeks.

"Don't get too excited. Meeting my pops ain't nothing special. He already know I'm a hoe." The way my face dropped was priceless. I was about to kick him in the dick before his father came in the room.

"Why she looking like that, son?" his father asked. He scrunched his face up at me.

"She told me she was excited about meeting you. I told her that was no reason to be excited because you knew I was a hoe. You meet every-damn-body," he repeated to his father. Both Kyson and his father were laughing hard as hell, and I was still trying to see what the fuck was so funny.

"What's funny though?" I finally queried.

"Damn. I see she got an attitude too. Just like your mother," his father stated.

"Yeah. I'm working on taming that ass," Kyson told him.

"Good. Give her some good wood, and it'll knock that attitude right out of her," his father mumbled. My mouth dropped again. They wanted my face to hit the floor and crack the fuck off from the way they were acting.

"Baby, we are just playing," Kyson informed me. The way they were laughing, it didn't seem like they were "just playing".

"Oh," was the only thing I could think to say. He had me so fucked up and so did his wrinkled-dick daddy. His father looked exactly like him and Kayson. His poor mother would've caught hell in the house with him. However, she would've probably given him the knowledge he needed to be sympathetic to his woman because the information he got from his father wasn't correct at all.

"Pops, this is wifey. This Mone't. Mone't, this my ol' man. We call him Pops. You might as well call him that too," Kyson told me. It felt weird as hell, but I was going to give it a try.

"Nice to meet you, Pops," I said in a low tone, extending my arm so we could shake hands.

"Girl, I don't shake no damn hands. I give hugs and rubs," his father commented, winking at me.

"Well, you won't be hugging and rubbing shit over here. You're my father, but I have no problem fuckin' you up," Kyson told him. We all laughed before we all stepped inside the kitchen. Kyson told me that we were going out to eat, but his father had already cooked, and the food was smelling good as hell. It reminded me of the big Sunday dinner they always had on *Soul Food. He must've invited the whole damn neighborhood over,* I thought to myself. We stood around talking for a minute before the kids came running into the kitchen. I was glad because my stomach was growling. I was past ready to eat.

The kids ran right to Kyson. It was nice seeing the softer side of them. He got down on his knees and allowed them to take turns jumping on him. He would stop to reprimand them when they became a little rough and explained to them that he wasn't fussing but that he was warning them to be careful to avoid someone getting hurt. I liked that about him.

"Ummm... Mone't," Kyson's father called me name.

"Yes?"

"You like older men? Kyson and I are the same."

"Naw. My mother told me old men give you worms."

"I'm sure she wasn't talking about no damn tape worms or something. She talking about that other big ass worm." He chuckled. I could see where Kyson got his slick tongue from.

"Mr. Pops, you do know I date your son, right?"

"And? I taught him everything he knows." He winked at me. I couldn't help but laugh at his crazy ass.

"I'm good. Thanks, though."

"I'm just playing with you. That's why you got something white on your clothes," his father said to me. I was embarrassed. It had to be dried up precum or some shit that flowed out of me while Kyson was fuckin' with me earlier. The way his father was looking and smirking at me made me uncomfortable. I'd never be able to look at him the same again. I was going to kill Kyson's ass.

"Daddy has someone for you to meet," Kyson loudly spoke to the kids. I wanted to clean myself up before he introduced me to them. There was no opportunity for me to do so since he was eager for me to meet them. I had to go with the flow. Luckily, they were young and wouldn't know what the white stuff was or where it came from.

"Who, Daddy?" the little girl asked him.

"This is daddy's girlfriend. Her name is Mone't. Mone't, this is Tamale' and Blaze. They are the light of my world," he introduced us.

"Is she your girlfriend like mommy was?" Tamale' asked him.

"Actually, mommy was never daddy's girlfriend. We lived together for you two," he told them. He was a little too honest with them if you asked me.

"It's okay, baby. You could've said yes," I spoke.

"Nope. I'm never going to be the one to lie to them. Ever!" I nodded my head in understanding before squatting down.

"Hello. You are very pretty," I told Tamale'.

"You okay," she said to me and rolled her eyes.

"Kyson, I know you fuckin' lyin'."

"Tamale', lose the attitude before I pop that ass," he chided.

"I'm sorry. Hi. Pops, can we eat?" Tamale' quickly apologized and brushed me off at the same time.

That little girl was going to be hell on wheels. I was sure she was a replica of her mother. She was going to be the first child I ever whipped because I wasn't going for that disrespectful shit. I knew she was having to learn a new woman and probably upset because she knew she was going to have to share Kyson's attention, but she legit had me fucked up. I'd fight a child. Her ass better think about all that attitude she was giving me.

"Where's the letter, Pops?" Kyson removed me from my thoughts to ask his father a question.

"In your room on the dresser," his father replied. Kyson got up and took off toward what I assumed to be his room. He could've taken me with him and given me a tour of the house or something, but he didn't. Instead, he left me standing in the room with his goofy ass father and that smart-mouthed little girl. I'd made up in my mind that I wasn't going to force her into building a relationship with me. I was going to focus on Blaze and building a relationship with him. Once she saw how good I was to her brother, I was sure she'd do better with wanting to bond with me.

"Fuck!" he bellowed when he returned to the kitchen. He was holding a letter in his hand. "When did this come?" he asked his father.

"What's going on?" I asked. I was very concerned. He was getting upset, and I didn't understand why. Not when we had a good day so far and he was just excited about me meeting the kids and us taking them out together to do something.

"These muthafuckas want to take my kids," he announced.

"Wait... Huh? Who wants to take them?" I asked, still confused with what was going on.

"These hoes from the child services place. They said something about a family member stepped up and wanted to take Tamale' and some dude saying he's Blaze's father wants to take him. How the hell can they do this? These are my kids!" he yelled.

"Baby, calm down. We need to call and see what's going on," I told him.

"We? Who the fuck is we? You don't even want anything to do with them. Ain't you a social worker? Your ass probably the one who located these folks so they could take my kids so you can have me to yourself."

Smack...

"Kyson, you got me so fucked up right now. I don't need a man that bad to do something as desperate as that. I'm glad I know how you look at me now. Take me back to my car so I can get away from you. This time, I want you to stay the hell away from me," I spat and walked out of the kitchen and into the living room.

The way I felt was indescribable. Kyson flipped on me just that quick. That was one of the reasons I never wanted to be involved with someone that had kids. There I was trying to be supportive of him, and he took it as me trying to separate him from the kids. That wasn't even the type of person that I was. For him to say those things led me to believe that he'd already been thinking that way and never said it. That was okay because his ass didn't have to worry about me anymore. He was acting like a true fuck nigga, and I had no problem treating him like one. His ass better ask Jared.

"Come here, Mone't." He came inside he living room, calling me to him. I flopped down on the couch and turned away from him. There wasn't shit he could say to me to change the way I was feeling. "Seriously, come here. I need you. I didn't mean to say those things to you. I was mad."

"I don't give a damn if your dick was on fire and the only way for the fire to be put out was for someone to tell you that you had to talk crazy to me. I'm not your enemy. You're right. I am a social worker, and although I may be young, I know a lot about child services because I worked there. Instead of being a fuck nigga to me, you should've been picking my brain to see what we could do about the situation."

"I know, and I was wrong. I swear I never meant to upset you. I'm not used to this relationship shit. I'm trying to get it right with you. I promise you I am. Please, help me keep my kids," he pleaded with me.

"I'm upset with you right now, Kyson. Can we talk about this later? All I want to do is go back to my hotel and erase the fact that this happened," I informed him, meaning every word of what I said. He apologized, true enough, but he'd hurt me. I was a firm believer of making a person feel the shit they did to me. If I had to feel the hurt, he was going to receive some type of backlash from it. I had to learn a long time ago that when a person crossed me, I had to handle their ass the first time to prevent the shit from happening again, and that was exactly what I was going to do to Kyson's ass... after I helped him find a way to keep the kids first.

8
KAYSON

Two Weeks Later...

Toccara told me that she was going to quit working at the pharmacy. It upset me because I would no longer be able to spend the time with her that I wanted. As much as I wanted to blame Bree for what happened, I couldn't blame anyone but myself. Toccara gave me a few chances to make shit right and to cut things off with Bree, but I didn't. She wasn't a good person, and her pussy wasn't that great, so it should've been easy. The only reason I wasn't quick to do it was because I wasn't in a relationship and I wasn't having sex with anyone else. Bree was someone I'd already been with, so I didn't think it would hurt to continue to sleep with her until I could find a replacement.

It was a Monday morning, and I was more than ready for the pharmacy to close. I went through an interview process to hire more staff, including another pharmacist. I needed to get my shit together and be prepared for Toccara to walk away from me. She had proven to me that she would cut my ass off at the drop of a dime, and that was what she'd basically done. She didn't answer any of my calls unless I texted her first and said it was work related. When we were at work and I tried to make small conversation with her, she would shut me down. She said the only time she wanted to talk to me was when it was work related. It killed me on the inside. She was hurting me, but I wasn't going to let her or anyone else know that. I didn't want to appear to be weak in front of anyone else.

"Ms. Jones, do you mind stepping into my office?" I called Toccara. I wanted to make things seem professional so I could get her to come into the office and talk to me.

"I'll be right back, Lauren," she said and came prancing toward me. I stepped back inside my office and took a seat behind my desk.

Toccara was a little dressed down today. It had me wondering if maybe she'd had a long weekend. I knew she couldn't have been doing much, because Mone't had been up under Kyson. The only way Toccara would've been busy was if she was with another man, and I wasn't having that.

Knock... Knock...

"Yes?" she stood in the doorway and asked. She was beautiful rocking a peach-colored spaghetti-strapped maxi dress under her lab coat with some peach-colored Chuck Taylors. It didn't matter if she was dressed up or down; she made anything look good. However, she pissed me off with that standing in the doorway shit. She would not step inside of my office for shit.

"I need to speak with you," I said to her.

"I'm listening," she replied. She still stood in the doorway.

"Come inside and shut the door."

"I'm good right here, Kayson. What is it that you have to say to me that you can't say from where I'm standing?"

"This is a confidential matter."

"I don't care. Violate my privacy. I'm not about to step foot in the place I saw you with that bitch," she spat. Instantly, her eyes became watery. She was finally on the verge of telling me how she really felt. That was what I wanted her to do—in private, not in the door where other people could hear.

"Fine," I blurted out. I stood from behind my desk, picked

up a folding chair, and headed for the door. "Follow me," I told her.

"Why? Where are we going?"

"You have a problem speaking to me about anything in the office, so I'll take you somewhere else. But to be honest, I'm really sick of this shit. You are acting childish as fuck, and you're too old for that."

"I wonder why..." she said under her breath, but I heard her loud and clear.

"Bring your ass on," I demanded. I'd allowed her to walk over me long enough. She wasn't doing the shit anymore. The one thing I learned from Bree was to not continue to work with someone that you have a strained relationship with. At this point, my and Toccara's relationship was very strained, and I couldn't take it anymore. I'd allow her out of her contract for her residency and help her pick one up somewhere else if I needed to.

"I'm not going anywhere if I don't know where I'm going."

"Toccara, if you don't bring your bald-headed ass on here, I'm going to drag you by those nappy ass curls in your head," I informed her. I hated to seem mean and rude to her, but maybe that was what she needed to fall in line because her attitude wasn't the best. Nor was it something that I was going to continue to put up with.

"Fine. But don't say shit to me unless it's work related," she whined. I tuned that shit out because I wasn't trying to hear any of the bullshit she was talking. I wanted to fix us, but only she would be able to tell me how to make it happen. If she didn't see by the way I handled that LeBron nigga that I was willing to do any and everything I had to do to make things right with her, then she was a damn fool.

Leading the way, I led her toward another office that was in the pharmacy. I kept that door locked all the time and acted as if I didn't have a key. It was actually bigger than the office that I was using and had a better view, but I kept my office because it had two ways to get in and out, and if I left out the back door, I'd be able to get to my car with no problem.

"What is this?" she inquired when I led her inside. It was fully furnished and set up the way an office needed to be. It was a lot neater and cleaner than my office. I leaned the folding chair that I had in my hand against the wall. The only reason I even brought it was because I wanted her to think I was taking her somewhere that might've not been so nice. It was my way of being petty and worrying her for no reason.

"What are you doing, Toccara? Why are you torturing me like this?" I asked her as soon as she stepped inside the office. I shut the door behind her. Taking her hand, I guided her to where there was an empty chair and assisted her with having a seat. It was shocking that she even allowed me to touch her. That meant something to me, even though I was still overly pissed at her.

"Torturing you? Are you being serious right now?" she replied curiously. The expression on her face showed concern, but the words coming out of her mouth were the complete opposite.

"Yes, I am. We had a friendship. You took that away. We worked good together. You took that away. I wanted to build a relationship with you, and you took that shit away too. What do I have to do to make this shit right?" I questioned her.

"At this point, there is really nothing that you can do. I'm done with the entire situation. I was going to quit, but I didn't because I wanted this too bad to quit. I appreciate all the things that you've done for me and for giving me a chance, but I'd really like it if you'd let me do my two years here without there being any more problems or confusion," she requested. Hearing her say that did something to me. I'd lost her and never even had her. *How the fuck did that even happen?*

"I'm not going to let you walk away from me like that. You're not doing that to me," I commented.

"You are not my father. You aren't fuckin', feedin', or financin' me, so don't get things twisted. I do what I want to do when I for that reason. If you knew you had to stick your nasty dick in any dirty bitch that came your way, then you never should've come after me. Now you fucked up and lost a good woman and want to blame the world. No. You need to look in the mirror. There's no one to blame but you and your lil' thirsty dick. Now move!" she hollered.

"Keep it down. We have customers," I reminded her, but she wasn't trying to hear anything that I had to say. She didn't want anything to do with me, and it was making me angrier and angrier. I could've strangled Bree's ass for putting me in this situation. If I would've fired her a long time ago, she wouldn't have had a chance to come near me. Fuck! This was all my fault.

"Fuck them customers and fuck you. I'm not playing with you. Move out of my way," she ordered again. She stood to leave, but I couldn't let her. I wanted her in the worst way, and she had to understand that.

"Don't say that, baby. You don't mean that. Please chill out," I pleaded with her before leaning in and sucking on her neck. Her body stiffened. She initially started trying to push me off her, but I wouldn't move. I was sucking on her neck like a bloodsucker. I was determined to leave hickeys on her neck, marking my territory.

"Stop, Kayson. You can't do this. You can't make me mad and try to kiss on me to make it better," she said just above a whisper.

"I only want to make you feel better," I advised her. She never responded. Her body relaxed as I moved around her neck, sucking and kissing on her. One of her dress straps fell down on her shoulders. I could almost look down and see her nipples peeking up at me on her beautifully perky breasts. I wanted to suck on them next. I continued making a trail around her neck before pushing my luck and moving down a little further until I reached her nipple. I peeked up at her to see if she was going to stop me. Her eyes were closed, and she was living in the moment. So I took my chances. I wrapped my lips around her want to do it. All that shit you're talking needs to stop becaus swear I don't want to hear it," she informed me. She seemed li a completely different person. She wasn't the same Toccara th came in there a few months back searching for a way to bett herself. She was hurt. She was confused. She was upset. Nobo could be blamed for any of that but me. It had me wondering she'd gone back to LeBron or if she was with someone el because of how hard she was going to try to get me to see th she was done with me. The only reason I didn't want to believ it was because I knew she was pissed with me and people woul say anything to get under your skin when they're not fucki with you.

"This isn't you. You don't act like this. You're better tha this," I fussed.

"Don't tell me what I am. You haven't been true enough t me to know how I really am. That could've happened if yo would've kept your dick in your pants." I stood in her face an looked down at her. She kept holding that mistake over my head. Something I'd apologized to her for over and over again. I tried to make things right, but being a woman, all she did was make things hard for me. *How could things get better between us if she wouldn't let them?* It was like she didn't want them to get better. That was something I refused to believe because I knew that we were meant for each other. If she'd let that hurt go, then we could move past all of this shit. She wouldn't. All she wanted t do was go off on me, ignore me, and find a way to either say o do things that were hurtful to me.

"That's the real issue, huh? You're mad because I fuck Bree? I could've did anything else but fuck another bitch, hu Why? You mad because I wasn't fuckin' you? You a whole virg and I'm a nigga with needs. How long do you think you could gone without giving up the pussy?" Nothing I said was mean wanted her to hurt the way that I was hurting, so I lashed ou

"Wow. Move out of my damn way, Kayson. You knew I w fuckin' virgin before you pursued me. I purposely made it kr

big, succulent left nipple and went to work sucking on it like it was a lemon. Soft moans escaped her lips. My dick started to stiffen up in my pants. It had been a minute since I had sex, but if she was willing to let me feel her insides, I was ready to do it. This might have been the wrong way to take her virginity, but it was going to happen. I was determined to be the one and only man to ever feel the inside of her, no matter how big of a fight she put up.

Toccara was so in a zone and feeling everything that I was doing to her. I couldn't stop there. I wanted to go even further. I planned to do as much to her as she would allow me to do. I brushed a hand against her leg to see if she would move it. When she didn't, I felt comfortable enough to go in for the kill. Pushing that hand up further, I managed to reach her panties. That was when she finally grabbed my hand, and her eyes popped open.

"What are you doing, Kayson?" she asked.

"Let it happen, baby. I'm not going to hurt you," I assured her.

"I'm a virgin, Kayson. I'm not doing th—" I placed my mouth over hers to keep her from speaking. I used my other hand to remove her hand from around my other wrist and pulled her closer to me. I noticed her eyes closing once more. That, to me, meant that she was relaxing again. She needed to remain that way.

With her hand still in mine, I guided it down to my dick that was waiting and ready. Her eyes popped open again when she had the chance to really feel how big it was. I removed my lips and smiled at her.

"I'm not going to hurt you," I promised her.

Making another trail, I moved back down to her breast and took her nipple back in my mouth before moving her panties to the side with my hand and using one of my fingers to begin massaging her clit. She proceeded to moan again. She shivered at my very touch. Toccara was wet as fuck. She was actually wetter than any woman I'd ever been with. Shit, if this was what it felt like to be with a virgin, then I should've stuck to breaking them in. Damn!

After a while, I added a second finger inside of her. I moved the two fingers inside of her while I used my thumb to continue to massage her clit. Her head fell back as she enjoyed the pleasure she was receiving. My fingers started to grow tired at a certain point, and I was tired of wondering what she tasted like. I removed my fingers from inside of her and lifted her up. Gently, I placed her down on the desk.

"What are you doing?" she curiously asked again.

"Trust me," I replied. That probably wasn't the best choice of words to use with her. I really needed her to trust me. If she did, then maybe I'd have a better chance of making her see that I really liked her and wanted to make everything alright between us.

"Trust is not something to be taken lightly, and you've lost mine. I'm leaving, so move." She was ruining the moment. I wasn't about to let her leave while she was upset with me.

"Toccara, look at me," I requested

"What?" She answered. Not once did she look at me.

"Look at me!" I repeated myself.

"I'm looking, and I don't like what I see. You are not the same Kayson that I caught feelings for. You're not the same Kayson that I trusted and respected. I don't know what I ever saw in you," she fussed, but I drowned her out.

Dropping down to my knees, I parted her legs and dove straight in. I placed my mouth over her clit and used my tongue to lick on it while I sucked on it like I was a vacuum cleaner. It wasn't long before Toccara shut the hell up. The once-soft, low moans that were escaping her mouth became loud screams.

"What are you doing to me?" she hissed.

Ignoring her, I continued to pleasure her with my mouth before deciding to allow my two fingers to reenter her. Her body bucked. She wasn't used to the feeling that she was receiving, and it was clear because of the way her body was reacting to me.

"Oh my God. Something is happening," she exclaimed. I smiled on the inside because I knew exactly what she was about to do. In my mind, I was telling her to go ahead and quench my thirst.

Toccara started moving her body to match the thrusts my fingers were giving her. She threw her pelvis forward and started grinding on my fingers and tongue. I stuck my tongue out further and allowed her to move her body the way she wanted against it. Within a matter of minutes, she let out one final scream, and her juices began flowing out. I clamped down on her pussy once more so I'd be able to enjoy catching all of her juices. It was so much that it started flowing down the sides of my mouth. I wasn't complaining at all, because she tasted as good as I always imagined that she would. When she was done, I used my tongue to lick her clean before standing up between her legs. I wrestled with my pants preparing to release the beast I had been holding in.

"Thank you, but that still doesn't change anything. Go brush your teeth and get back to work," Toccara instructed me. She stood from where she was sitting, fixed her dress, patted me on the shoulder, and headed for the door.

"What the fuck! I just ate your pussy, and you gon' up and leave like ain't shit happened? You played me," I muttered, dumbfounded that she was doing me like that.

"Naw. You played yourself, homie. At least now you know what real pussy tastes like. Have a fabulous day and remember to not say shit else to me unless it's work related."

Toccara had me fucked up. I was livid at the way she allowed that shit to go down. *Who the fuck even thought to do someone like that?* That was petty as hell, and she wasn't going to get away with it. My dick was hard. My heart was pounding. My mind was racing all over the place. Something had to be done. I had to find a way to get my girl back.

9
TOCCARA

The day went by so slow. I couldn't wait to call Mone't to tell her what went down. I wanted to call and tell her about it from work, but I couldn't, because there were too many ears around. Was I wrong for the way I handled things with Kayson? I probably was, but I didn't care. He deserved that for the numerous times he gave me hope that we would see where things could go between us, yet constantly did shit that left me with hurt feelings.

"Have a good evening, Lauren," I told her as I grabbed my purse and headed for the door.

"Toccara, please leave your key and badge when you leave," Kayson told me as I twisted the doorknob to leave.

"What?" I quizzed as I turned to face him. "What the hell are you talking about?"

"I refuse to be in another uncomfortable work environment. That's the same shit I went through with Bree, and I'm not about to do it again. It causes too many problems," he explained.

"It causes too many problems for who? I don't have a fuckin' problem. I'm good."

"See? I haven't cussed at you one time, and look how you're coming at me. Our relationship has run its course on a personal and professional level. I'm sorry." He turned and walked away without giving me a chance to respond. There was no one there but Lauren, Kayson, and me. Of course, Lauren stood there as things played out because she was nosey as hell. She probably had her phone out recording everything because she was the type of bitch that would run and tell anybody's business but her own—those unhappy bitches.

"You are not about to do this shit, Kayson. It's not right. I haven't done anything to you. You mad because I won't pursue anything further with you? That's your fault. When I tried, you were too busy with your pussy-eating lips sunk into Bree's ass. You mad because I let you taste the pussy and left you with a hard dick in your hand? Again, your fault. I didn't ask you to touch me. You mad because I won't give you any pussy? Your fault because you knew I was a virgin. You want me to strip naked in here and let you fuck me on top of the box of Percocets that just came in? What do you want from me?"

"If he doesn't want to fuck you on the percs, I'll definitely take you on this case of Ativan that just came in," Lauren hollered out of nowhere. I knew that bitch was gay. Ignoring her, I kept my eyes trained on Kayson.

"I want you to let that shit with Bree go. We weren't in a relationship. I didn't cheat on you." Technically he was telling the truth, but it still didn't change the fact that I was hurt by seeing him with another woman. He needed to be able to understand things from my perspective too. "Toccara, I'm not telling you to forget what I've done. That's something I know won't happen because of everything you've had to go through like the fighting and going to jail. That was all due to the decisions I made. I get that. Not once did I not acknowledge that I messed up. I know I did. Give me credit for trying to fix things. That's all I want. Let me do what I gotta do to fix it. Stop punishing me for the same thing over and over again. You can't live your life punishing people for shit they did in the past. Humble yourself. Accept their apology. Forgive, but don't forget."

"Don't try to preach to me, Kayson. Who are you to tell me what I need to be doing when you couldn't tell yourself to keep your dick in your pants?"

"You wasn't saying shit when I didn't keep my tongue in my mouth earlier."

"Damn. So y'all nasty, nasty? Go 'head on Boosie Badazz and Big Latto," Lauren cracked. Both Kayson and I hit her with the side-eye, and she hurried to shut her mouth. "On that note, I'ma go ahead and head out. Can you lock the door behind me?" she stated to me.

"No, because I'm coming out the door with you," I told her.

"No you're not. You're staying in here until we work this shit out," Kayson commented.

"Boy, bye. You not my daddy."

"I didn't nut to create you, but I will be nutting in you. You will forgive me, we will get married, and have kids. You might as well stop all that bullshit you doing right now."

"I have a date. I'm out," I told him and walked right out the damn door. I made sure to slam it behind me. The pharmacy wasn't big at all, so he didn't have those sliding doors. Plus, we always left out the back door where we had to park so it was a regular door there. It didn't take much for me to slam the bitch.

"Don't slam my fuckin' door, Toccara. Come back here when I'm talkin' to you." I could still hear him screaming as I left out the door and got in my car. I cranked it up and flipped him off before speeding out the parking lot. It caught me off guard when he blew a kiss at me. That nigga was crazy. It had me wondering what the hell he was going to try to do next.

When I'd gotten away from the pharmacy and headed toward my house, I connected my phone to my car so that I could call Mone't. We needed to talk. It had been two weeks since we saw each other, but we spoke as much as possible. It almost felt as though Kyson was keeping us apart, but I knew he was doing his best to help her deal with everything that was going on with her. Bree and I had to drop charges on each other the same way that she and Mone't had to drop them. The last I heard, Bree was still in jail because LeBron was still keeping his charges against her for bumping him. I knew he was doing it for me, but he didn't need to. There was no way I'd ever give him the time of day again.

Picking up my phone, preparing to call Mone't, I received a notification on my phone that I had a new friend request. It was from a guy named Javonte' Crockett. I glanced at his picture and liked what I saw, but I didn't know him, so I closed out of the app and proceeded to call Mone't like I initially planned to do.

"Hey, boo!" Mone't answered.

"Girl, I have to tell you something. Can you come over?" I announced.

"I wish I could. Kyson is dealing with something major right now, and he needs me. I have to be there for him like he was for me."

"Damn. I get that he your nigga, but you trippin'. You just done threw me away, hell." I didn't want to sound insensitive, but I was annoyed. How the hell she go from hanging with me all the time to not having any time to spend with me at all? The shit was ridiculous. *Was my friend allowing her man to change her?*

"I'm sorry, Toccara. I promise as soon as this is over, we are going to spend a lot of time together. What's going on? What have you been up to? Why can't you tell me what it is over the phone?"

"Because I wanted to see your damn face when I told you. Damn! I didn't know I needed an explanation to talk to my friend."

"Come on, Toccara. Don't be like that. I told you that Kyson had something going on with him. I'm trying my best to be there for him the way he needs me to be. He was there for me, so it's only right that I be there for him. You know that. Why are you tripping with me?"

"I don't know. Maybe it's jealousy. I want to be happy too, Mone't. You don't think I deserve it?"

"Of course you do, boo. You deserve to be happy and not to have to settle. You're giving the situation too much control over you and becoming a person that you never were. You're very moody, and you snap on any and everybody. You remember how your mother used to always tell us that if you allow other people to dictate your mood, you're giving them your energy and it weakens you."

"Yeah, but it's hard. I'm trying my best to let this shit go, but it's hard when he won't leave me alone. Then he called himself firing me today. What kind of shit was that? It was wrong as hell for him to do that to me."

"Yeah. He's being an asshole. Bless his thottie little heart. Forgive him, Toccara. That's the only way you can get past this. That man wants you, and he's sorry. He was wrong, but he really didn't cheat on you, boo. I know you don't want to hear that, but I'm always going to be honest with you. If you want to be with that man, then let that shit go and try to make the shit happen. You're getting older. You want to be happy, and he's the one to do it."

"Maybe so. I don't know. Probably not after what happened today."

"What happened?"

"Girl, I let him eat me out. When he thought he was about to dip inside of me, I dipped out on his ass."

"Bitccchhhh... You did what?" Mone't hollered out, laughing at me. I couldn't help but laugh too.. "Why would you do that?"

"I didn't ask him to do it. He just did, and it felt good, so I didn't want to stop him. I needed some type of sexual contact hell. Look how old we are, and I've never been touched by a man."

"Yet you had a whole damn near-death experience when you tried to use the rose that time."

"Mind your business, bitch," I barked at her. That hoe didn't forget shit. "You get on my nerves. You're always bringing up old shit." I giggled.

"I miss you too, bitch. Make this shit right with Kayson, sis. I promise you won't regret it. Now, let me get off here and go see about Kyson. I'll call you Friday so we can go out and have a girls' night. Love you, sis."

"Love you too, bitch!" I beamed, hanging up the phone with no other words spoken.

As I was getting ready to put my phone down, I noticed that I had a message request from the Javonte' guy. My curiosity mixed with the fact that I knew I could read what he said without him knowing that I read it urged me to open it.

Javonte': Hello bu2ful. How r u?

Who the fuck spells some shit bu2ful? I thought. I knew what he meant, but damn. It had me wondering if all of his words were spelled in a funky way. I didn't have time to be trying to sit and figure out what he was trying to say. That was when I went to his profile picture to see if he looked how he sounded. Dumb.

Pleasantly, I was surprised. The brother had it going on. From his pictures, he looked like he could've been six feet even. One picture that caught my attention in particular was one where he was wearing some gray sweats, standing inside some building and pointing up to the sky. Of course, he didn't have a shirt on, so I was able to get a great view of his athletic build, abs, and tattoos strategically placed along his beautifully sculpted caramel body. His face contained high cheekbones and very little facial hair. He did have a small mole under his left eye. It wasn't big at all and actually added more detail to his facial features. He was definitely somebody I could stop and stare at all day long. His hair was in a low-cut fade, and he had diamonds in both of his ears. There wasn't shit else going on with me so hitting him back was not a problem.

Me: I'm good. How are you?

Javonte': Wow. I neva thought u would reply. U r so sexy.

That message caused me to blush. It also caused me to go back to see if we had any mutual friends. It would be suspect as hell for him to up and reach out to me out of the blue. When I checked, I did notice that we had at least five mutual friends. That wasn't bad, but I was expecting more.

Me: How did you find me?

Javonte': Ur name came up as ppl I may kno. When I saw it, I wanted 2 get 2 kno u better. Is that a problem?

Me: I guess not. Are you single?

Javonte': I'm whateva u need me to b.

Me: Hmmm... That sounds suspect. You can't answer with a yes or no?

Javonte': Yes, I can. Being simple takes away 4rom the mystery. 2 answer ur question... Yes, I am single. No kids. Own car. Own job. Own house. What's up?

Me: Me too.

Javonte': Do u mind if I take u out on a date sometimes?

Me: Let's get to know each other a little first and then see what happens.

Javonte': Bougie I c.

Me: You must be blind because I'm far from bougie. Anywho, I have something to do, so I'll talk to you later.

There was really nothing at all for me to do, but he was getting on my nerves. We hadn't talked about much of anything, but I was thinking a lot about what Mone't said. Maybe I shouldn't have responded to Javonte' and went back to talk to Kayson to see if there was anything we could do to really work things out. My mind was all over the place. Things would've been so much better if I knew what I really wanted.

Ring... Ring... Ring...

My phone began to ring. It was Mone't. She told me that she had some shit going on with Kyson and I respected that. I didn't answer because I felt like I might have made her feel guilty and that was the reason she was calling. I didn't want her to feel that way. She didn't deserve that from me or anyone else.

Ring... Ring... Ring...

Mone't called my phone back to back. That was one thing we

always did to each other. When one of us called the other and they didn't answer, we'd keep calling until we got a busy text or an answered phone call. Being who I was, I went ahead and sent Mone't a text to let her know that I wasn't going to answer. She deserved to be happy, and it was evident that Kyson was giving her that happiness. Who was I to get in the way of that? All I wanted was for her to make sure she was really happy and to not rush into anything. I made a mental note to talk to her about that whenever we did have our girl's night out.

Me: Sis, deal with your man. If I made you feel bad earlier, I'm sorry. I love you, and we will talk some other time.

Sis: Bitch, get to the hospital now. There was a fire at the pharmacy. Kayson is hurt.

Slamming on brakes, I damn near hit a curb trying to make a U-turn in the middle of the street. What the fuck was she talking about? I hurried to call her back because that wasn't something for her to be playing about.

"Toccara, you need to be answering your damn phone. There was a fire at the pharmacy. I don't know the details. All we know is that Kayson was inside. He was rushed to Singing River Hospital via ambulance. Kyson cutting the fuck up on the folks because he thinks Kayson will die at that hospital," she informed me.

"Please tell him to calm down. I'm on my way," I voiced and ended the call.

My heart was racing. I felt like I was about to have a damn heart attack. My head began pounding with worry. I closed my eyes and began praying. That was the only thing I could think to do at the moment.

10

KAYSON

"Move out of the way. I need to get to my son." My pops' voice rang out loud as hell inside the emergency room. All I could do was shake my head. He was concerned about me, yet he was embarrassing me at the same time. Why couldn't he show concern without showing the fuck out?

"Sir, we can't let you in there until we make sure he is fine," someone told my father.

"Bitch, if you don't move, I'll shut this whole fuckin' hospital down. I've been his legal guardian since he came out this ball sac. Where is he?"

"I'm in here, Pops," I returned. All I wanted him to do was shut the hell up before he got put out the hospital. Then I would have to leave because there was no way in hell I was going to allow my father to get put out and do nothing about it. That would've been hella disrespectful to me, even though it would've been his fault the reason he was kicked out.

"Where?" he yelled.

"I'm in here," I said again. The curtain flew back, and Pops came rushing to my side. Grandpa Robert was with him.

"What the hell happened, son?"

"I honestly don't know. None of it makes sense. I was in the office trying to finish some last-minute paperwork so I can be off over the next few days. All of a sudden, the lights started flashing on and off inside the building. Shit had me thinking that I was losing my mind. I got up to go see what was going on and was hit in the back of the fuckin' head. I was out for I don't know how long. I'm not sure how the fire started or when. I was awakened by a firefighter only to see smoke covering the building. I was glad they came when they did because I could've died in there," I explained to them.

"I'll be damned. Who would want to hurt my boy? I'm going to kill the muthafucka who did this to you. You still got those cameras set up in there?" Pops asked me.

"I sure do. I'm glad you reminded me. I need to call the security company to get them to check them and send me all of the footage from tonight. You think I'll need a warrant from the police to get that information?" I probed.

"Why would you? It's your company. You can call and get anything that you want when it comes down to that pharmacy," my grandfather chimed in. I was about to say something to him about what happened between him and Kyson. However, the expression on his face told me that he didn't want to talk about it in front of our father. He knew just like I did that Pops would chew his muthafuckin' ass out if he knew what happened.

"I dunno. I've never had to call them for anything like that before. I'll do it as soon as I can."

"You'll do it as soon as you start feeling better. And what's all that shit they got in your nose?"

"They are giving me oxygen. I inhaled some of the fumes from the smoke. They want to make sure things are okay with me, Pops. I think they are going to keep me a few days to run some additional tests to make sure everything is okay," I explained to him.

Knock...

A black woman came in wearing scrubs. She was sexy as fuck,

but she wasn't Toccara. She was wearing her hair in a bob. I could see that it wasn't really her hair, and I hated that. I loved natural beauty, and she wasn't giving that to me at the moment.

"Y'all plan on keeping my boy in here?" Pops asked without giving the woman a chance to explain who she was or why she was there.

"We most certainly are," she replied to my father.

"What's the prognosis, Doc?" Grandpa Robert asked.

"That's not the doctor. Shut up, Robert," Pops fussed at Grandpa Robert.

"Actually, if you would let me talk, then you would know that I am the doctor. I'm Dr. Craig, and I'm the attending physician for the ER tonight," she explained.

"What you gonna do about my boy?" Pops queried.

"We have run a few tests on him. Some that we have results for and others we are still waiting for. Because he was in the fire and smoke inhalation is dangerous, we are going to keep him possibly for the next two days to monitor him. Then he'll be able to go home," Dr. Craig told my family.

"How long will it be before he gets taken to a room? I'm going to run grab some clothes so I can stay up here with him," Pops announced. My eyes darted up from my phone and over to him.

"What you mean? I'm not a child," I ranted.

"And? This is Singing River Hospital; I don't want you dying up here."

"You say that about every hospital."

My brother and I were born at this very hospital, the hospital my mother died in while giving birth to us. For that very reason, my father hated hospitals. This one specifically. He'd drive to Africa if he could to avoid having to go there. Everything going on with me was serious, so I couldn't bypass being brought there. Besides, I'd never had a bad experience, so I was fine with them taking care of me.

"You have always been crazy as hell. Don't nobody want your

big ass staying with them. He a grown ass man," Grandpa Robert chimed in. "He needs a woman in here with him. Doc, you got any single nurses?"

"On that note, I'm going to step out. As soon as your room is ready, they will transport you up," Dr. Craig stated before leaving out of the room.

"I can't take y'all anywhere. I'm going to be fine. I need someone to go by my house and pick up a few things for me," I advised them.

"Can't you call your brother? He ought to be good for something," Grandpa Robert spoke. I knew he was throwing shade, and I was honestly tired of it.

"What the fuck is that supposed to mean, Robert?" By the way Pops raised his voice, I knew he was already on ten about Grandpa Robert's comment.

"All I'm saying is Kyson always in some shit, and someone has to step up to get him out of it every single time. He's too old for that."

"All you saying is bullshit. That boy hasn't gotten into any trouble since he got out of high school. He's stepped up to be a man in every single way. You don't have room to talk about anybody when you can't even keep your dick in your pants. Now, you can do me a favor and go to hell because I will not allow you or anyone else to disrespect either of my boys." Exactly what I thought. Pops went smooth off on his ass. Grandpa Robert kept his mouth shut because he knew damn well he wasn't a match for Pops.

"Y'all doing too much. I'm leaving since you got everything under control. If you need anything, call your grandmother. Don't call me," Grandpa Robert emphasized.

"You don't have to worry, I won't," I told him.

"I sure as hell won't," Pops added. Grandpa Robert dropped his head in defeat and exited the room. "Let me call your brother and update him on what's going on. I'm going to be right out here if you need me."

"A'ight."

As soon as they were both gone, I picked my phone up again. All I wanted to do was call Toccara and let her know what had happened. I needed her. Bad. It was sad that she couldn't see how sorry I was for hurting her.

Ring... Ring... Ring...

My phone began ringing. When I glanced down at the screen and saw that it was Bree, I sent her straight to voicemail. I wondered how the hell she was still calling me when her ass was supposedly still in jail. Shit, she was broke, so she didn't have any money to bail out. Let her tell it, she didn't have family that wanted anything to do with her. It had me curious as hell but not enough to want to talk to her.

Ring... Ring... Ring...

No matter how many times I declined her call, she kept calling back. She was about to be blocked. It was getting ridiculous.

Knock...

"Everything okay in here? You know your phone is ringing, right?" a nurse came in and asked. I was about to say something to her ass because I was tired of them knocking one time and walking in the room. They don't even give me a chance to say come in before they entered. That was rude as hell. Both the doctor and nurse did it, so maybe that was a policy they had or something. If it was, they needed to change that. I could've been in there with my dick out. I started to ask her how many people she walked in on fucking because that one knock clearly didn't give anyone enough time to get themselves together before the folks walked in on you.

"Yes, it's fine. Do you know how much longer it'll be before I'm sent up to a room?"

"It won't be too much longer. I'll go see what the holdup is, and I'll be right back," she informed me. I noticed her winking at me before she left out of the room. I ignored it because I wasn't about to engage in anything further that could cause me even more problems with Toccara's crazy ass.

Ring... Ring... Ring...

"What do you want, Bree?" I finally answered after seeing how relentless she was with calling.

"I wanted to call and check on you. Are you okay? What are they saying?"

"I am not any of your concern. How'd you know something was wrong with me anyway?"

"That doesn't matter. Are you home? Do you need me to come to you?"

"Bree, did you do this?" I probed, figuring she would lie and say she didn't.

"Are you okay, Kayson? I'm trying to be a good girlfriend right now." She did everything but answer my question.

"A good girlfriend? I don't need you being anything for me. All I need for you to do is leave me alone. You get that? Leave me the fuck alone, Bree!" My phone was placed right at my mouth when I said that because I wanted her to hear me loud and clear. That "girlfriend" shit she was talking about was dead. She couldn't be dumb enough to really think we were together.

"Kayson, why won't you let me be there for you? Is she there?"

"Yeah, I'm here bitch, and don't you forget it!" Toccara's voice sounded off in my ear. It startled the hell out of me. My back was turned to the door, so I never saw her come in. She didn't even knock.

"I gotta go. Don't call me again," I hollered into the phone before hanging it up.

"Oh, I see your lil' girlfriend was checking to make sure you were good. I can leave, and she can come up here," Toccara told me. If I hit women, I probably would've tried to smack her for saying that dumb shit.

"Don't play with me. What are you doing here anyway?" I quizzed.

"Mone't was with Kyson when he got the call, and she called me. I came right over here because she didn't have much information to give me. I was scared."

"Scared for what? You said you didn't want anything to do with me."

"Me not wanting to be with you on that level doesn't mean that I don't want anything to do with you at all. You should understand where I was coming from. All of this has been hard on me. I'm a drama-free person. Ever since I met you, all I've had was drama, and I can't deal with that. The fighting. The arguing. I grew out of that shit in middle school. You should understand that," she explained.

"I get it. I've never tried to bring drama into your life. I'm not a person that deals with drama either. The drama that I have in my life is because of Bree's crazy ass, and I've done everything to erase her from my life. That was why I fired her."

"You fired her and turned around and fucked her," she interrupted me to say. "It doesn't even matter. We aren't together, so you're free to do whatever you want," she continued.

"Don't say that. Let's talk about this."

"I'm not here to talk about that. I'm here to check on you. If you want to keep talking about that, then I need to go ahead and leave." Leaving was the last thing that I wanted her to do. It was good to be in her presence and have her at least talking to me. The fact that she came showed me that she had some care for me. That was good.

"Oooo..." I howled out in pain.

"What's wrong?" Toccara ran up to me and grabbed me. She wanted to see what was wrong.

"I don't know. A sharp pain shot through my chest," I lied.

"Okay. Let me get the doctor."

"No. Don't leave. I'll tell them about it when I get to my room. If I tell them now, they are going to try to keep me down here longer, and I really want to get settled. Will you stay with me tonight? I don't want to be alone," I honestly admitted to her.

"I really don't think that's a good idea. I'll stay with you until they move you, and then I'm going to leave," she concluded. It crushed me that, even though she was there with me, it still felt like she was being cold and distant. I hated that. I wanted the Toccara back that I first met. The carefree Toccara that showed care and concern for everything and everybody. She was the type of person that would see a possum in the road and slam on brakes instead of hitting his ass. If it was up to me, I'd speed up and have the possum hanging on to my rims for dear life.

"A'ight," I simply replied, hoping to save face.

"How long are they keeping you anyway? You seem to be fine to me."

"They said they were going to run a few more tests on me and I should be out of here in two days."

"Two days? Why would they keep you two days for some tests? Did you ask them what kind of tests they were? If everything is perfectly fine with you, then you should be able to go tomorrow." It was unclear if she was showing concern or fussing at that point.

"Let me find out you care," I teased.

"I never said I didn't care about you. What you did was fucked up. I'm not dealing with you on that level right now."

"Right now? So you're telling me that somewhere down the line, I may still have a fighting chance for you? For us?"

"I don't know. Right now, I'm not on that. You need to see what's really going on with you."

"There's nothing going on. I'm telling you that they are running tests to be safe."

"And I'm telling you that's a damn lie. Come on, Kayson. We aren't doctors in the medical sense. However, we are pharmacists. We've had to research a lot and take a lot of medical-like classes. Think of some of the terminology they have used. Does it really seem like they are keeping you for two days for some damn tests only?" The more she spoke, the more I thought about what she said. She was right. It didn't make sense. Wanting to ease her mind and mine, I hit the call button to ask for them to send the doctor back in the room. It seemed like Dr. Craig must've been standing right outside the door because she came marching inside the room in a matter of minutes. She didn't even bother to knock this time. I wanted to say something, but Toccara beat me to it.

"Who are you?" she asked Dr. Craig.

"Oh, I didn't know anyone was in here with Kayson," she announced.

"You didn't have to know that someone was in here to have been taught that you always knock on someone's door before you enter. What? Were you expecting to get a free look at his dick or some shit?" Dr. Craig immediately began blushing.

"She didn't mean that, Doc," I chimed in.

"Yes the fuck I did. You don't speak for me. I meant everything that came out of my mouth. We may not be together right now, but I'll be damned if I'm going to let any other trout-mouthed bitch think they have a chance to take my place," Toccara scolded. I wasn't even sure where that came from, but it had me scared for a minute. Toccara was acting throwed the fuck off. I'd never seen her act that way with anyone other than Bree. The shit kinda turned me on.

"Baby, calm down. Let's ask her all the questions you have so then you'll feel more comfortable about me staying here," I suggested to her.

"I don't need to ask her any questions, because you're not staying here. You'll stay in my parents' basement with me before I allow you to stay in here with these damn Peeping Toms," Toccara continued ranting and raving. It was quite flattering. Yet the shit had me worried that she was about to set it off in this fuckin' hospital.

"I can assure you that I abide by my code of ethics, and I refuse to get into a relationship with a patient. I only came in here to let him know that he was about to be transported to a room."

"Are you getting smart?" Toccara asked. She stepped up like she was about to hit Dr. Craig. I hopped down out of the bed to get between the two.

"Baby, you said I could stay with you before I stayed a night here, right?"

"Yeah. Whatever," she rebutted. What the hell was going on? How could she offer me a place to stay one minute and trip out on me the next? I wasn't her damn enemy. If anything, I was the one trying to bring peace and happiness in her life. Things just hadn't worked out the way I'd like for them to.

"Come on, Toccara. Let's sit down and finish our conversation," I told her. That was my way of trying to take her mind off Dr. Craig. It seemed like she was going to rip her head off her shoulders at any given moment.

"Why you keep telling me to calm down and shit? You trying to protect her like you did that bitch, Bree? I will not stand for you putting another woman before me again. You hear that?"

"Yes, baby. I promise that's not what's happening here. She's the damn doctor. I don't want her," I expressed.

"Well, damn. Tell me how you really feel," Dr. Craig blurted out. What the fuck she do that for? It almost sent Toccara off on the deep end.

"What you mean by that? I already you told you that he was off limits, but this ass whooping not," she fussed.

"Yep. She's gonna beat that ass," I co-signed.

"You damn right I will. I don't give a fuck if you work here or not. I'll drag you out of this hospital by your damn nappy ass roots."

"Straight drag your ass," I added.

"You better let that bitch know that I molly wop bitches as a sport. Don't play with me, ma'am. Kayson is off limits," she spoke.

"Definitely off limits," I reiterated.

"Kayson, your X-rays came back, and there is a mass on your lungs. We need to do a biopsy to make sure it's not cancer," Dr. Craig blurted out. I wasn't sure if her ass was playing or not, but now wasn't the time for fuckin' jokes. Especially not jokes like that.

11

BREE

Very intently, I listened to Kayson and Toccara's conversation. He was damn near begging her to give him something that I had been trying to give him since the first day I laid eyes on him. Thinking back to the day I saw him for the first time, I was in heaven.

Kayson's grandfather had hired me right out of high school to work for him. He only hired me because I went to him crying about needing a job. It wasn't like I was lying. My mother put me out right after I graduated. She said she was tired of my attitude and me coming in her house anytime I wanted. She found it disrespectful and told me she was no longer going to tolerate it. The day she told me about it, I was very upset and lashed out at her to the point that I almost jumped on her. That wasn't fair to her, considering all the things she had done for me to make sure I graduated on time. She wasn't wrong. I'd been acting crazy with her since I was eleven, which was the first time I experienced sex. The guy was twenty. I lied and told him that I was eighteen. It was easy for me to get away with because I wasn't built like an average eleven-year-old. That was a story for another day. However, the things that man did to my body were undeniably things that I wanted to continue happening. So I was hot in the ass, trying to get that feeling from whoever, whenever, and wherever I could get it. My mother knew. She was disgusted because she didn't raise me like that. There was nothing she could do to stop me, which was why, the minute I turned eighteen and graduated, she tossed my black ass out on the streets.

The day she put me out, I was walking down Main Street and came upon the pharmacy. I always remembered my grandmother going in there to get her medications and telling me how nice the owner was. She told me he was a black man that helped her out plenty of times when she couldn't afford her medication. That piqued my interests to go inside to see if he would be nice enough to hire me. Talking to him was easy. All I really had to do was laugh at his corny jokes, poke my ass out, and bat my eyes. Of course, he was intrigued and offered me a job. Having my own was something I couldn't wait to rub in my mother's face.

For the first few months of being out on my own, I was basically homeless. I had to bounce from house to house, staying wherever I could to make sure I had somewhere to sleep at night. The minute I'd saved up enough money to get my own place, I did it. I moved in with an air mattress, some candles, and some canned goods. That was all I needed to get me to my next paycheck so that I could get all of my utilities on in my name. It was crazy how the lights weren't on in the apartment. I thought they kept them on and all I had to do was transfer them over to my name. Ashiiidddd.... These people must've been burned by a tenant before because they didn't have shit but the water going, and that was only because the water bill was included in the rent.

By the second week of me working at the pharmacy, Kyson and Kayson came trotting inside to visit their grandfather. They were both sexy as hell, but Kyson's mouth was too slick for me. He probably was the one I should've gone for, but I didn't. I knew I wouldn't be able to run over him. I at least felt that I had a better chance of getting over on Kayson. You see how that turned out for me. Their grandfather introduced me to them, and neither of them spoke. That should've been enough for me to walk away, but I didn't. They were too fine for me to not get a word in with either. Kyson and his grandfather happened to walk to the back. That was my opportunity to speak with Kayson. He was very dry with me, but that didn't matter. We spoke, and I felt I left an impression on him that would draw some form of interest in me. It worked because as soon as he took over the pharmacy, we couldn't keep our hands off each other.

"Aye, where you at?" my new man called out to me. I hurried to hang my phone up. Prayerfully, nobody heard him talking. I couldn't remember if I'd put the phone on mute or not while I was trying to listen to their conversation.

"Ugh, I'm in here," I replied right as he entered the bedroom. He came straight over to me and planted a sloppy kiss on my cheek. I hated that shit. *Who the hell gave people wet kisses on the cheek?* It wasn't sexy, and it sure as hell wasn't cute. I was sure my face scrunched up when he did it. Luckily, he wasn't able to see it.

"Why you acting suspect?" he pulled back from me and asked.

"Suspect? What you mean?"

"You were all jittery and shit when I walked in here. What were you doing?"

"Nothing, baby. I was on the phone, trying to find another job. I called an agency to see if they were hiring. You walked in right as the phone started ringing, so I hung up before they answered," I lied.

"Bree, do you see the time? Ain't shit open this time of night but gas stations, hospitals, and a bitch's legs. Don't fuckin' lie to me," he spat.

"Baby, I'm no—"

Smack...

Out of nowhere, he smacked me. It wasn't the first time he'd done it. It had been happening since the day that he brought me home with him. I should've walked away from him then. I couldn't. With no job, there was no way I'd be able to keep my apartment or car and pay my other bills. He offered to help. That was something I couldn't refuse. Hell, he was my knight in shining armor. Meeting him was a blessing for me. At least, it was what I kept telling myself.

While I was in jail, I agreed to drop any charges I was going to and had already pressed on Toccara and Mone't. Yet they wouldn't let me go because that LeBron dude lied and said that I'd hit him. There was no proof of it. It was his word against mine. I couldn't afford a real attorney, so I had to settle for the public defender. That didn't do anything for me but get a bond set. It wasn't something I could afford, so that meant I had to stay in jail until I went to court again or until LeBron decided not to pursue anything further. The way my luck was set up, there wasn't a good chance of that happening for me. Or so I thought.

"Let me out of here. I didn't do anything," I cried and kicked on the cell bars.

"Shut up, bitch. You in here like the rest of us. Don't be making all of that noise, because we don't want to hear that shit," one of the ladies in the cell with me said.

"Fuck you! I can do what the hell I want," I spat. I was sick of people telling me what to do. I wasn't a weak bitch. She was going to be the one that I had to make an example out of.

"Hey! Keep it down in there," a deep voice said. That was when I looked up and locked eyes with him. JC was everything to me. He was tall, dark, and handsome. Well, minus the dark. He wasn't finer than Kayson, but he was still fine. The sound of his voice turned me on. I wanted him to touch me in the worst way. Not being able to get a nut with Kayson earlier, I was still very much so horny.

"Can you help me?" I asked when he neared the cell I was in. He got close enough for me to reach out and touch his face.

"Why are you touching me?" He briskly took a few steps back. I was angry that he was turning away from me because he was my only option at that point.

"I really do need your help."

"I can't help you. I come to work to do my job and go the fuck back home. I'm not trying to help anybody do shit so I can be in here sharing a cell with them."

"You wouldn't even help little ole me?" I asked, moving my hand up

to my mouth and sucking on one of my fingers, attempting to be flirtatious with him.

"That's not going to work. I get more pussy than a single woman with a bunch of kids gets in food stamps. I don't need to risk my job trying to help somebody who don't have shit to bring to the table."

"How do you know what I can bring to the table? You don't know me," I fumed.

"Check this out... You have a little ass bail. All you need is five hundred dollars to bail out, and you can't pay it. That's a problem. That means that you probably searching for a man to take care of your ass, and that ain't me, shawty."

Dropping my head, I felt defeated. That was really the first time that a man rejected me. Kayson didn't count. His rejection was only because he was trying to save face with Toccara's ass. Had she never come into the picture, everything between him and me would've been fine.

"Fine. Go."

JC didn't think twice about me telling him to leave. He quickly turned on his heels and prepared himself to walk away.

"Please! Help me!" I loudly whined.

"What you want me to do? I'm not paying your damn bail. I don't even know you. You'll probably dip the hell out on a nigga if I try to help you out." That was when he turned and left. Two more days passed, and he still wouldn't help me out. I was about to be transferred to the detention center when a different public defender finally came and to talked to me. I explained to her what happened, and she said she would do what she could to help me. That led to me having a meeting with LeBron. He was so mad at the way that Toccara curved him for Kayson that he asked me to help him get back at her.

At first, I told LeBron I wouldn't mind helping him. It wasn't until I told him he was going to have to pay me for my services before I decided to help him out did the shit backfire on me. He thought about it, so he said, then came back and told me he changed his mind about needing my help. In my opinion, that nigga didn't want to pay me. He was going to do what he could to get revenge on both Toccara and Kayson on his own. But he did go ahead and drop the charges against me. He knew just like I did that when Toccara saw me freely moving about, that was going to get under her skin more than anything. LeBron's ass didn't even bother to give me a ride when I was released. I ended up bumping into JC, instead. I had to give him head in the parking lot in order for him to give me a ride. He was supposed to take me home, but he never did. Instead, we ended up at his house, where I'd been ever since I was released from jail. I regretted the shit each and every day.

Several times a day, I checked Toccara and Kayson's social media pages to see if they were together. Not seeing any posts indicating that they were a couple, I held out hope I could get him back. I reached out to him from different numbers hoping he would pick the phone up, but he never did. I hated that Kayson was one of those people that didn't answer the phone when he didn't recognize certain numbers. The one time he did answer, it was when I called from my number. If I had known he would answer for me, I would've called him from my phone a long time ago.

"Now you acting deaf. You don't hear me talking to you?" JC stood in my face yelling. Spit was flying out of his mouth, and he had veins popping out of his forehead. The shit was quite scary.

"I hear you. I was letting you finish talking before replied," I lied.

"What I say then?"

"What you mean?"

"What did I say if you heard me talking to you?"

"Why are you trying to pick a fight with me? Why do you always have to put your hands on me?"

"Enough. I'm sick of your mouth. Take your clothes off. I'm going to fix your ass."

Most people would be hyped about what he said. He was about to beat my back in, right? Wrong! JC was crazy. He respected nobody but his mother, father, and cross-eyed ass sister. I often wondered if any of the women he dated called the police on him for abuse. Did he even abuse them? We never talked about his past, but he knew a lot about mine. I thought he asked about my past because he really wanted to get to know me. I was wrong. He was gathering information he could use against me at a later time. That was how he was able to get and maintain mind control over me.

Daily, he would tell me how nobody wanted me or loved me. That he was the only person that could handle being in my presence. I used to think I was the prettiest woman to grace this earth, but he took all of that from me. Yes, in two weeks, he had broken me and killed my self-esteem.

Whap...

"Didn't I tell you to take your clothes off?" He appeared enraged. I didn't want to take my clothes off. I feared what he was about to do to me. Apparently, I was right for having that fear.

"JC, stop. Please! We can talk without you putting your hands on me," I pleaded with him. My tears flowed down my face as soon as he hit me. My back stung underneath my clothes. It felt like it was on fire.

"What the fuck did I tell you to do? When I was talking to you, you came at me with that smart-ass mouth. I'm not that Kayson nigga. You not going to be talking crazy to me."

Whap...

"Take that shit off now," he demanded.

"No!" I tried to stand my ground.

"Oh, you talking back now?"

Standing from where I was once sitting on the bed, I did my best to get past him. He roughly pushed me back on the bed and began tugging at my clothes. The loud sounds of them ripping could be heard throughout the room.

Whap... Whap... Whap...

Repeatedly, he lashed at me with his leather weight belt. The pain was excruciating. I knew he was going to kill me all because I didn't want to take my clothes off. It was my choice. I had a right to say no. That was what they always said in those damn movies and shit. Why was he trying to silence me?

"Let me leave. I won't tell anyone what happened," I cried, begging him to let me go. My cries fell upon deaf ears. He didn't hear shit I had to say.

Whap... Whap...

It was like he was in a zone. The whipping was so intense. One would've actually thought that I'd really did something to deserve what he was doing. I didn't. He was acting like my father and not my man. I couldn't take it any longer. I had to get away from him. He was going to kill me. The only thing I thought to do was play dead. No matter how much it was hurting me, I stopped crying. I wouldn't even move. I lay there stiff as a board.

"Get up, Bree."

Whap...

"I know it ain't shit wrong with you. Get your muthafuckin' ass up."

Whap...

"Okay. You want to play? I got something for your ass," he bellowed. My eyes were open so I could still see his every move.

Quietly, I watched as he marched toward his top dresser drawer. I knew what he was going to get out of there. We engaged in a lot of freaky shit. He had to be grabbing a dildo. Probably the biggest one we used. I hated it because it hurt like hell. Still, I didn't move. When he turned to come back my way, he was carrying his taser and the dildo. There was no way he was going to do what I thought he was going to do.

"You still want to play I see. I'm 'bout to show you how I'm not the nigga for you to be playin with," he muttered.

The moment he turned the taser on, my eyes bucked. He was really going to stick me with it. I couldn't allow that to happen. The closer he got to me, the more nervous I became. I had to do something. When he was close enough to me, I drew back my leg and kicked him between his.

"Urrrggghhhh... You crazy bitch. I'm going to kill you," he seethed. He grabbed his balls and immediately dropped down to his knees. That was my chance to run, and I did just that.

Running for the door, I grabbed the robe that he always kept hanging near it and his wallet, then took off running out the door. Not stopping to look back and with no destination in mind, I kept running. Somebody was bound to find me and help me out. As long as it wasn't JC, I didn't care. I had to get away from his ass and for good. No matter how much people hated me, I didn't deserve this. I deserved to live. The whole time, Kayson remained on my mind. Getting back to the love of my life was all I thought about. JC and Toccara may have been obstacles in my way, but I would walk through fire to get back to Kayson.

12

KYSON

By the time Mone't and I made it to the hospital, they had rolled Kayson up to a room. Toccara was standing outside in the lobby waiting for us to come so she could direct us to where the room was.

"Thank you for coming, Toccara. I'm sure that meant a lot to my brother," I told her. Toccara had been stubborn as hell about talking to Kayson and working to get things right. She knew like everyone else that they were a match made in heaven. Yet she was a woman. She wasn't going to allow anything to be easy for my brother. Not after she felt like he'd purposely hurt her.

"It's no big deal. I need to tell you something," she told me.

"Tell me what?" I was waiting for her to tell me that they had worked things out. Then I paid attention to her body language and facial expression. Something was wrong.

"Nevermind. I need to let your brother tell you. It's his business to tell." Whatever it was, it had to be big. She appeared worried.

"Naw. Damn that. Tell me what the problem is. I've gotten enough bad news to last me a lifetime. If something is up with my brother, then you need to tell me now." I reached out and roughly grabbed Toccara by the arm. I yanked her closer to me and glared down into her face.

"I know you fuckin' lyin'. Take yo' muthafuckin' hands off my sister before I beat your ass in this hospital," Mone't snapped. She grabbed me by the back of the neck. I wasn't sure what came over me, but the thought of something happening to my brother really had me fucked up. What could she have been keeping from me?

"Tell me what is going on," I demanded through clenched teeth. I bit down on my jaw a few times. It was so hard that I could feel the blood as it ran into my mouth.

"Get your damn hands off me," Toccara ordered and snatched away from me.

"And if I don't?" I retorted.

"If you don't take your dick-beating, pussy-fuckin' hands off me right now, there won't be shit left of this hospital but rubble. That's how bad I'm going to beat your ass," she told me.

"And I'm going to help her," Mone't co-signed. I laughed. They needed to sit their crazy tail selves down somewhere

It took some time, but I thought about what was happening. Not responding to Mone't or Toccara, I walked over to the registration desk. Toccara was acting like she didn't want to tell me shit, and I wasn't about to beg her. If she wanted me to talk to Kayson about whatever it was, there was no reason for me to delay doing so.

"Good evening, sir. How may I help you?" the dude at the receptionist's desk asked me.

"I need to know what room y'all moved my brother to." I gave him his name and tapped on the desk, impatiently waiting for him to respond.

"Kyson, come here. I need to talk to you," Mone't advised me.

"Hold on. I'm trying to find Kayson," I told her.

"I'm going to show you how to get to the room. Stop being an asshole for once, Kyson," Toccara interrupted.

"No. I'm not about to beg you for shit. You could've told me what the hell was going on. Women have to be so complicated. I'm not doing this shit with you," I grunted.

"Kyson, she is trying to show you. You can keep being a dick all you want and talk about what you're not going to do now. I guarantee you're not going to like it when I tell you what I'm not going to do later," Mone't assured me.

"What is that supposed to mean?"

"Figure the shit out."

Mone't walked away from me and went to take a seat in the nearest chair she could find. My head immediately began to hurt. The way she was acting was uncalled for. She had to understand what I was feeling. My pops kept calling me and saying everything with Kayson was going to be fine. Now, Toccara saying that she had something to tell me, yet she wouldn't tell me. She kept telling me that I needed to talk to Kayson because it was his business to tell. She should've known that was going to make me worry. The shit didn't sound right. Mone't getting mad at me for displaying my feelings was ridiculous.

"What are you getting mad for? It's not your brother."

"I understand that. I want you to know that the way you are acting is uncalled for. You think this is only stressful to you?"

"Why wouldn't it be? She wasn't even checking for my brother before his shit happened?"

"You don't know what I was doing. Men like to go stick their dick in a hole in a tree and want women to act like they didn't do shit. You and your brother got me fucked up," Toccara muttered.

"You acting like he cheated on you," I rebutted.

"It's not about him cheating. To y'all, he may not have cheated. I get that. Yet he came to me about wanting to see where things could go with us. In the midst of that, he thought he was going to keep creepin' with the bitch from his past. How can you build something for your future when you keep holding on to the past? If he could sleep with her before we really started our relationship good, who's to say that he wouldn't sleep with her while we were in a relationship? That type of shit is alarming. You don't get it, because you're thinking with the same fuckin' head he's thinking with. His mufuckin' dick," Toccara snapped. There wasn't shit I could say, because I got where she was coming from. It made sense that she would feel the way that she did.

"I'm not about to talk about that with you. All I want to do is see my brother and find out what's going on," I stated to her.

"Then stop being a dick to me and let me take you to him. You could've been in his room by now if you weren't so busy being an asshole. Now let's go," she scolded and marched away. Mone't jumped out of her seat and followed right behind her. I was right on their heels to avoid them getting too far ahead of me. All I needed was to get lost and be back where I started. No damn where.

The more we walked, the more the feeling of being in the hospital became eerie to me. It wasn't one of my favorite places to be. Honestly, I didn't want to think about the last time I had to be at one. That was the night of Cyn's death. Mentally, I knocked on wood and prayed that I wouldn't have to go to another one any time soon. Hospitals signified death and sickness to me. Those unhappy thoughts weren't something that I wanted in my head.

We weren't walking long before we got on an elevator. It was quiet as hell. Even Toccara and Mone't weren't talking to each other. That wasn't something that normally happened. The silence between us caused me to worry even more. *What is happening?* I thought.

Ding...

The elevator stopped and I waited for the ladies to walk out first. Toccara led the way since she was the only one who knew what room he was in.

"Move. I can do this shit myself." We could hear Kayson

yelling at someone. I picked up my pace and damn near jogged to his room.

"What is going on in here? What the hell are you doing to my brother?" I asked once I'd busted inside the room.

"I'm trying to help your brother change into his gown," a male nurse announced.

"The hell if you will," Toccara blurted out. "Get the hell back. That nigga not crippled. Fuck outta here," she added.

The nurse smacked his lips and prepared to leave. He reached the door and turned back around. He walked over to the dry erase board that was hanging in the room to write some shit down.

"I'm Adrian. I'm going to be your nurse for third shift. Hit the button if you need anything." After rolling his eyes a few times and giving Toccara the evil eye, he pranced out of the room.

"Damn, bruh. You ain't been here a few minutes, and you 'bout to get turned out," I joked, trying to ease some of the tension that was in the room.

"Kyson, don't catch these fuckin' hands," Kayson advised me. He never even cracked a smile.

"A'ight. Damn! What's going on? How are you feeling?"

"First of all, hey to your rude ass too. All of y'all."

"My bad. Hey and all that other shit. You good?"

"I'm coolin'."

"What the fuck is that supposed to mean? What is going on with you that Toccara acted like she couldn't tell me about?" I got straight to the point.

"Damn. If she told you something was going on, she should've at least told you what it was," Kayson stated to me before focusing his attention on Toccara. "You couldn't wait to tell somebody, huh? What? You hate me that much that you want me to die?" he snapped.

"Kayson, fuck you! I don't dislike anybody enough to put out so much negative energy that I would wish death upon them.

Furthermore, yeah, I did tell him that something was going on with you. Why wouldn't I? He's your damn brother. No, I didn't tell him what it was, because that's your place to do. If I had a dick, I'd tell you to suck it right now. Funky ass," Toccara retorted. "I'm out. I'm not dealing with this dumb shit," she announced.

"Don't leave, Toccara. You know what I'm going through. Show a little support here," he pleaded with her.

"Wow. There is no question that you are twins. You both do the same dumb ass shit. Talk to people crazy, and when they get ready to stop fuckin' with you, you want to soften your approach and get them to act like ain't shit happened," Mone't chimed in.

"Shut up. Ain't nobody ask you shit," I told her.

"Oh, no worries. I plan on keeping my mouth shut for a while," she indicated. That meant that she wasn't gonna give me no head. Hell naw. That wasn't going to work.

"Baby, I'm just playing with you." I chuckled. Moving closer to her, I pulled her in to me and began placing kisses all over her.

"Get off me, Kyson. I'm not 'bout to play with you." Mone't pushed me off her. I wasn't worried. I knew all I had to do was get her home and clamp down on that pussy. Once I had her ass singing like *The Temptations,* she'd be back to talking to me in no time.

Out of nowhere, Toccara's phone started going off. It was that same dinging sound that my phone made when someone would reach out to me via Facebook Messenger. She kept checking her messages and replying with a big ass cheesy grin on her face. She was talking to another nigga. I wasn't dumb. She was making the same face I would make when I was preying on another bitch. That hadn't happened since I got with Mone't, but it sure as hell was happening with Toccara's ass. I made a mental note to talk to her ass about the shit later. It didn't sit well with me that she was standing in my brother's hospital room and disrespecting him by talking to another nigga.

"What's going on, bro?" I asked Kayson, trying to take my mind off what Toccara was doing.

"It's nothing major. They keeping me so they can run a few more tests on me. Everything is going to be fine."

"Keeping you for how long? They couldn't have run all these damn tests while you were in the emergency room?" I probed. There was something he wasn't telling me. We were twins. He must've forgotten that our senses clicked and we always could tell when something was wrong with each other.

"There ain't nothing wrong. I'm telling you what they told me. They want to keep me for two days so they can run more tests."

"Your ass is lying. Don't make me go out there and call Drake's ass back in here," I threatened him.

"Who the hell is Drake?" he quizzed. Even Toccara and Mone't glanced up at me. They all looked lost and confused.

"The lil' flamboyant ass nigga that was trying to see them ass cheeks clap," I teased. That was me trying to lighten the mood even further because clearly something was up.

"Fuck you, Ky. Ain't nobody seeing this ass but Toccara," he stated.

"Apparently, Bree's been seeing it too," she squealed.

"I said I was sorry and I fucked up. I'm not going to say it no fuckin' more. Let the shit go, or you can leave," Kayson spazzed out on her. It was like Toccara wanted to keep hurting. If something really affected her so bad, why would she keep bringing it up so it'll continue to hurt her? She wasn't trying to let the shit go. What the hell was she even still coming around for if she was going to keep being childish like that? The shit was stupid. He knew it. She knew it. We all knew it.

"Fine. Don't say anything else to me," she grunted.

"Don't worry. I won't. I'm sick of the shit. You gonna keep beating on a nigga while he down? You obviously aren't the woman I thought you were. You can leave," he commented. Toccara's face dropped. Mone't was looking down the entire time, taking everything all in. When she heard Kayson tell Toccara to get out, her head flew up. She looked like she wanted to kill him. I shook my head. That was my way of telling her to stay out of their business.

Kayson was my brother, and I was going to side with him whether he was wrong or right. Even though I didn't like the way that he spoke to Toccara, I understood why he did what he did. Anybody would get tired of someone bringing up their past. It wasn't too long ago that the shit happened, but it wasn't yesterday either. Let the shit go and move on.

"Cool. I'm leaving," Toccara announced.

"Good. Go!" Kayson chided.

"I'm not playing. I'm about to walk out that door. When I do, don't call me thinking I'm going to come back."

"I don't want you to. Take your unhappy ass on. You want to continue to hurt and not let me try to fix the shit and make you happy, then do it on your own. You're dismissed," Kayson said. He clapped his hand a few times like Money Mike did on *Friday After Next*. I couldn't help it. I busted out laughing. His ass was goofy as hell.

Pop...

"It's not funny, Ky." Mone't scolded me right after she popped me on the arm like I was a child. That shit hurt.

"Damn, ma. You heavy handed as fuck. Keep your hands to yourself."

"No worries. I plan on keeping a lot to myself." There she went with those threats again.

"I let those lil' threats you are making slide the first few times. I'm not going to keep letting that shit go. Do what you need to do."

"Let's get out of here," she told Toccara. They intertwined their arms together and left out of the room. I shook my head because the entire situation was dumb to me. I got that Mone't and Toccara were best friends. At the same time, I felt like they needed to mind their own business when it came to certain shit.

It seemed like Mone't was jumping down my throat because of what was going on with Kayson and Toccara. She acted like I could control my brother and the way he acted. That was far from the case. Hell, I was the oldest, but his ass never listened to me. Even as children, I damn near had to box Kayson out to get him to do something I wanted him to do.

"I have to be honest with you, Ky. The reason I'm having to stay the extra time is because they found a mass on my lungs. I don't know much about it. All I know is that they want to do a biopsy tomorrow to see if it is cancer or not."

"What! How? This is not a time to be funny, Kay."

"I'm not being funny. I'm telling you that is what they told me in the emergency room because Toccara and I were both wondering why they would want to keep me for so long when I wasn't in the fire long enough for the smoke to do major damage to my lungs."

"This is some bullshit. I don't know what I would do without you. Fuck cancer! Rest in heaven, bro."

"Damn, Ky. You killing me before we know what's going on. How the hell you going to tell me to rest in heaven?"

"My bad. I don't know how to deal with all of this. If I could take somebody out and get their lung for you, I'd do it."

"The hell you will. I don't want nobody else's lung. They probably ain't even take care of their shit. Let me gon' to glory before you take shit out of somebody else's body." He was talking out the side of his neck. Let something happen and he couldn't make decisions for himself, I was the next in line, and I was going to sign every paper there was to get him a new lung. There was no way I'd be able to go on without my brother. I meant that shit when I told him that.

Toccara and Mone't leaving put us both in a stressful situation. We didn't speak on it, because we didn't want to add any more problems to the list of shit that we were already dealing with. Deep down, I knew he wanted Toccara to stay at the hospital with him. Since she dipped out, I wasn't going to allow him to be there by himself. Not with what he'd just found out about his health. I made a quick call to Pops to let him know what was going on and took a seat on the sofa that was in the room. I was glad he agreed to stay with the kids while we figured out what was going on with Kay. I didn't give a damn what anyone said, I wasn't leaving out of that room until Kayson did.

13
MONE'T

Toccara and I hurried to get the hell away from the hospital. Thankfully, she was in her car. We hopped in and jetted out of the parking lot. We decided I was going to stay with her for a while to play catch-up on everything. The first thing we did was stop at *Krystal* to grab something to eat before stopping by the hotel for me to gather some clothes for at least a week, and then we headed to our final destination. Initially, I didn't want to go there, because I knew Kyson's ass was going to come find me. He was so crazy at times. His ass would probably try to drag me out of the house by my damn hair, if he felt he could get away with it.

Entering Toccara's house last night, I could tell that she was drained. I was too. The events of the day were too much to take in. Kyson and I were still dealing with the letter he received about the family wanting to get custody of the kids and now this.

"Sis, you okay?" Toccara asked me, removing me from my thoughts.

"Yeah. I'm fine. Are you okay?" I replied. Truth be told, I was worried.

"Of course. I'm glad to know this is finally over and done with." She paused. "I need you to do me a favor."

"Sure. What is it?"

"I've blocked Kayson and Kyson from my phone. When I say that I am done, I mean that. It's going to be hard, but it has to be done."

"What about your residency at the pharmacy?"

"What about it?"

"Girl, you have to complete it. You've dreamed of this your whole life."

"I know. It's not the end of the world. I can do it. I'll just do it somewhere else. I'm actually thinking about leaving the state."

"What you mean?"

"I mean that I don't want to be here anymore. Mississippi is my home, and I'll be forever grateful for the memories I have here, but it's time to say goodbye. I've been thinking about it for a while. Tonight gave me the confirmation I needed."

"Wait... So you're going to walk away from your family and best friend all because a nigga doesn't know how to treat you? I don't get it," I muttered.

"It's not all about that," she chided.

"Then what is it? Help me to understand the shit," I yelled.

"Keep your voice down. My parents can hear you," she yelled back.

"How are you going to tell me to stop yelling and you start yelling? That sounds silly as hell," I barked.

"Mone't, this has nothing to do with Kayson. It has everything to do with me. When that shit happened with you and that video, you was ready to jump ship and go to Dallas. Everything in my life is not where I expected them to be right now. I need a change. I'm not walking away from our friendship. I'm not walking away from my family. I'm doing what's best for me. You're my best friend. Even if you don't agree with it, respect it because I would do the same for you." She was right. When I wanted to leave, she was sad and begged me to stay. However, she didn't judge me for wanting to go. She was never negative to me about it. She respected my decision. As her best friend and sister, I needed to do the same for her.

"You're right. I'm sorry. It's the fact that things have started to go right in my life. I'm happy with Kyson, most of the time. I'm starting my own social services agency, so I don't have to go back to work for anyone else. All I wanted was for my best friend to be around to enjoy it with me."

"Mone't, I'm not going to always be there physically, but my presence will always be with you," she assured me.

Toccara and I shared a hug. That was our way of apologizing to each other. We knew where our hearts were. We were both going through things on our own and needed to be a united front instead of arguing about something we couldn't control. We parted ways and prepared ourselves for bed. When we were done, we climbed inside of Toccara's bed and watched reruns of *Wild 'n Out* until we both had fallen asleep.

The Next Day...

Toccara was still sleep when I woke up. I didn't bother to wake her, because I knew she had to have been tired with all the shit that was going on. I did leave her a note to tell her that I had to go meet Kyson and that I would talk to her about what was going on later. Since we talked, I hadn't gotten a chance to tell her what was really going on with Kyson. It wasn't like it mattered. There was nothing she could do to help. She already had enough on her plate.

"We have to make this quick. I gotta get back to the hospital," Kyson told me as soon as I opened his door and slid in on the passenger's side.

"Yeah. Whatever."

"Don't start, Mone't. I don't feel like dealing with your attitude."

"Don't tell me what you don't feel like dealing with if you aren't going to take the time to see what the hell I feel like dealing with. Shut up and drive." My expression was stern so he could see that I meant business. It shocked me that he did what I said instead of trying to talk back to me as he always did in the past.

With me being a social worker, I knew a lot of people. That included people that worked for the Department of Family and Children Services. I hit up one of my old coworkers and let her know what was going on. She wasted no time looking the kids' information up in the system and giving me what I needed for the people that were claiming they wanted custody of them. Kyson and I called them and asked them to meet with us so we could try to get this situation solved. They quickly agreed. Something seemed fishy about the whole situation. I told myself I wasn't going to tell Kyson my thoughts or let him know that I was questioning everything until once we'd had a chance to meet them and I was able to confirm my suspicions.

Kyson drove like a bat out of hell trying to get to the hibachi Chinese restaurant off Highway 90. It was a crazy place to meet, but that was where they wanted to meet, and they wanted Kyson to pay for the shit. Naturally, he agreed because at this point, he was willing to do any- and everything that he could to maintain custody of the kids.

"You ready?" he asked as soon as we pulled inside the parking lot.

"Yeah. Let me start off the conversation. I'm a social worker, so I know the terminology to use that'll get across better to them."

"Fuck them niggas. I'm 'bout to threaten to put a bullet in their mufuckin' heads to let them know I'm not the nigga to be playing with," he barked. He had to let his ego kick in and start acting crazy instead of being man enough to let me coach him through the shit.

"Fine. Do it your way. I'll sit there and shut my mouth. I guess you had me tag around to look pretty on your arm, huh?"

"It's not like that. I want this to be over with. I don't need this shit hanging over my head. I don't understand why these mufuckas didn't step up before or why they didn't feel the need to help Cyn's crazy ass out when she needed them."

"They may be trying to get something out of the situation. You never know. That's why I told you to let me start the conversation. I need to get a good read on them."

"Fine. But you need to know that if this shit starts to go left, I'm handling it. Deal?" He stuck his hand out for me to shake in agreeance. Since I didn't want to argue with him any further, I went ahead and shook it so the conversation could cease.

After the handshake, he maintained control of my hand. We walked inside the restaurant hand in hand. It wasn't packed, so we were showed to a table immediately. Kyson was a nervous wreck, so he just sat there. My greedy ass got up to get something to eat. I wasn't passing up no food. Not no free food at that. By the time I made it back to the table, there were three people, two men and a woman, sitting in front of Kyson. His arms were crossed over his chest, and his mouth was poking out. It was cute and sad at the same time.

"Hi. I'm Mone't. I'm Kyson's girlfriend. You are?" I set my food down on the table and extended my hand to shake theirs. Neither of them said a word. They sat there and stared at us.

One thing I wasn't going to do was argue with them or try to fight them in a public place. I learned my lesson after the shit with Bree. If anything, I wanted us to be able to sit there and talk like adults. Since nobody wasn't saying anything, I sat by my food and proceeded to eat.

"So y'all ain't hear my girl talking to y'all?" Kyson sat up from leaning back in his chair. I rolled my eyes because I knew the conversation could go left. Kyson played about a lot of things, but the kids and I were two things he didn't play about. He didn't tolerate disrespect of any kind, even if his ass was the one giving the disrespect majority of the time.

"We heard her," one of the men finally spoke.

"Then open your mufuckin' mouth and speak back. Don't disrespect my girl. That'll get you fucked up, quick."

"Are you threatening us?"

"I don't make threats. I make promises and guarantees."

Kyson and the man spent some time going back and forth with each other. I sat there and listened in case I needed to jump up and defuse the situation. All they were doing were exchanging words. If it became physical, I wouldn't continue to let it slide. It went on for at least ten minutes. I'd gotten tired of it and finally had to say something.

"Okay, that's enough. We are here about the kids."

"What are you here for? You ain't got shit to do with this?" the woman spoke up to say.

"I'm his girlfriend. That means if he keeps the kids, they are going to be a part of both of our lives. What's important to him is also important to me, and that includes the kids. So you're wrong; I have everything to do with this," I explained to her.

"You really don't. I'm not going to argue with you. We are too grown for the foolishness," she added.

"Bitch, you got me so fucked up right now. I know you older than the damn *Civil Rights Museum*, but I'll whoop your old ass if you don't come at me better than you're coming," I warned her. I wasn't playing either. That bitch might not have liked me, but she was sure as hell going to respect me.

"Pardon me!" She threw her hand up to her mouth as if she were stunned by my reaction. She'd better be glad that was all she got because I had no problem fighting a single soul.

"We not 'bout to do all that. Tell me what y'all want. It can't be the kids, because neither of you have been there for them since the day they were born." Kyson got right down to the issue. We sat there in complete and utter silence, waiting for them to give us their answer.

"I want money. You can keep the kids. We had a little family event, and people were talking about what happened to Cyn and how the kids were given to you. I learned that you had a little money, so they thought the kids were going to be well taken care of. I don't let any opportunity of a come up pass me by, so when I heard about it, I instantly reached out to Stan to let him know what was going on. Blaze is his son, and he has a right to be a part of his life," the guy spoke. He introduced Stan as Blaze's father so that meant that he and the woman that was with him were the family members that wanted Tamale'.

"He don't have a right to do a damn thing if the only reason he is planning to be in his life now has everything to do with the fact that y'all think I have money. I ain't got shit. I'm a brother going out there every day working and hustling to make it," Kyson expressed.

"We've seen your house. We see how you be having the kids dressing and shit. The social worker probably didn't tell you that when she has you bring them up there for those so-called 'check-ins' it's because they are giving us a chance to visit with and bond a relationship with them, did she?" the man boasted. That didn't sit well with me. Those visitations weren't supposed to happen without Kyson knowing about it. Knowing him, he was going to do everything in his power to stop the visits.

"Let's go. I'm not sitting here for this dumb shit. I'm not giving you a dime," Kyson barked. He grabbed my hand and damn near yanked me up from where I was sitting. He was upset. I got it. That didn't mean he needed to dislocate my arm because he was mad.

"We will see you in court," I told them and held my phone up.

"You were recording us?" Stan jumped up from his seat and asked.

"Do birds fly?" I stuck my tongue out at him and kept walking. The recording might have been inadmissible in court because they didn't agree to being recorded, but I didn't give a damn. It could still be used as information to give to Estelada about what was going on.

Kyson tossed a twenty-dollar bill on the counter on our way out the door. That was to cover the cost of my food. He must've changed his mind about paying for their shit. I didn't blame him. If they wanted to be about money, their asses were going to have to find another come up because we weren't it.

14
TOCCARA

One Week Later...

Javonte': U fine as fuck, ma. I can't wait until we go out.

Me: Thank you 😘

Javonte': No thanx needed. The only thing I need is u.

Each time Javonte' messaged me, I found myself blushing harder and harder. He was a smooth talker. I enjoyed it. We had talked so much that I decided I would give things a chance and go out on a date with him. Especially since I was now fair game.

The night Kayson showed out with me at the hospital, I gave up hope that we'd be able to work things out. He'd done more than enough to make me be done with the entire situation. It was crazy how someone could hurt me without even trying to. Kayson had a lot going on with the mass and finding out what was going on with the fire. He really didn't have time to focus on anything else. That was fine. I got that.

At this point, I didn't want to know what was going on with him. If I said I was done, I needed to show that I was done and stick behind my words. If I continued to say it and then show up every time he called me, I was sure to keep falling back into the same cycle with him. I didn't want that. That was why I blocked him and told Mone't that I didn't care what she learned about him, keep it to herself. She agreed. That was perfect for me.

Javonte' and I had continued to maintain contact with each other. The more I talked to him, the more I started to like him. He asked me to go on a date with him, and I agreed. I told him it would have to be somewhere out in the open. He said he was fine with it. I also made it clear to him that there would be no sex involved. We hadn't exactly had conversation that was sexual, but I did make it a point to let him know I was a virgin and planned to keep it that way until I found the one for me. It was sad how I'd thought about giving myself to LeBron and Kayson only for them to show me their true colors. I was thankful for the fact that I moved slow in the dating arena because it allowed me to weed out who would or would not be good for me.

"Where are you going?" Mone't waltzed inside my room while I was getting dressed.

"I told you I was going out on a date."

"A date? A date with who? I didn't know you were dating anyone," she spoke.

"I'm not technically dating him. I've been talking to him for a few weeks," I replied.

"A few weeks? Where did you meet him at? How do you know him?"

"I met him on Facebook. Don't laugh. I know it sounds silly. He actually reached out to me."

"Bitch, haven't you watched enough episodes of *Catfish* to know that you can't trust these folks? You are randomly messaged by a guy on Facebook that you've never met or never heard of, and you're willing to go out on a date with him? Have you checked to see when the profile was created? Did you see who his mutual friends were? Let me see a picture. We need to run it through Google image search to see if those are really his pictures or if he pulled them from another website." The way that Mone't was acting was why I didn't tell her much about what I had going on. She was going to overreact the way she always did. She was making this out to be a big deal because she said she was concerned. However, I knew it was because she wanted me to work things out with Kayson. If it wasn't him, she couldn't see me being with anyone else.

"Calm down, Mone't. I checked all that stuff out. I even had Olivia inbox him to see if he would try to holler at her." Olivia was the sister I was closest too. She laughed about it when I told her everything too. That was really the only thing I did do. I told Mone't I had him checked out when I really didn't. I was too busy trying to find someplace else to do my residency at to do a background check on the damn dude. The best and quickest thing I could think to have done was get Olivia to go after him to see if he would try to talk to her.

"What happened?"

"He shut the shit down. That's the only reason I agreed to go on this date."

"Maybe he saw pictures of her on your page and knew who she was. He would be a fool to get caught up in something as easy as that." That was something I hadn't thought about. I did post a lot of pictures on my social media sites, so it wouldn't have been hard for him to identify that Olivia was related to me. Damn. Had I fucked up by agreeing to go on this date?

"Let me have a little fun, Mone't. You and Kyson are always doing shit. You don't have much time for me anymore. Let me try to go out and find the love and happiness that you have," I argued with her. Shit, I was tired of everyone else around me being happy while I was sitting in the house like a damn stuffed potato all the time. That was exactly what I was going to look like if I kept sitting in the house all the time because all I did was eat.

"I get that you want happiness and a relationship, but that is not something you rush. You have to take your time and let that man come to you. The same way we did with Kayson and Kyson. I know you're mad at him, but I still have hope that things are going to work themselves out."

"I'm glad you have that hope because I don't. When I told you that I was done, I meant that shit. The way he acted at the hospital was more than enough for me to walk away from him for good."

"I swear you have always been as stubborn as a damn mule."

"And? What's your point?"

"My point is that you need to quit being a peppermint patty, get your man, and let him have your ass bent like a pretzel. I promise once you let Kayson put that dick in your life, all that animosity is going to go right away," Mone't teased me.

"Girl, bye! He ain't sticking shit in me that he put in Bree. I'm cut from a different cloth. He fucked a bitch that smelled like horse shit. Ain't no telling where else he's had his musty dick." I was talking crazy. I wasn't sure why. Ever since I allowed him to taste me, I dreamed about him being inside of me. I couldn't let that happen. It would never work.

"I hear you. Where are you going on this date? What's the guy's name? What does he look like?" Mone't shot off question after question. I knew she wasn't going to drop the issue, so I had no choice but to answer her.

"His name is Javonte', and like I said, I met him on Facebook. Here is his picture." I pulled out my phone and went straight to his page. At least I tried to. My phone had to be tripping because it wouldn't go to his page. It was as if the page never existed. I never even saved a picture of him. "That's strange."

"What's strange?"

"My phone isn't pulling up his profile. See if you can do it on your phone?"

Mone't handed me her phone, and I put Javonte's name in. Nothing came up. I scratched my head in disbelief because I'd just seen the page a few minutes ago. We were messaging each other. That made me go to Messenger to pull up our messages. They were gone too. This couldn't have been happening.

"What are you going to do?" Mone't asked.

"I'm meeting his ass at the *Applebee's* in Ocean Springs. I want to know what the hell is going on," I aggressively spoke. I was furious. Had he tried to play me? Whatever it was, his ass wasn't going to get away with it.

Earlier, I was excited about the date. I found this cute dress in the back of my closet that I'd never worn before that I was going to wear, but damn that. I chose a pair of ripped jeans, a polo shirt, and my Nike Air max. I was prepared to fight him if I needed to. He was about to give me answers on what the fuck he had going on.

"You can't be serious about still going on this date."

"Like hell if I'm not. Toss some clothes on because you're going with me," I instructed.

"Oooo... You know I'm always down to beat a nigga's ass. Give me a second, and I'll be right back," she told me and ran out of the room.

While she was away, I threw my hair up in a ponytail. I applied light makeup to give the illusion that I was trying to pretty myself up for him. I was classy with a bit of hood, and my attire showed that.

Ding...

My phone notified me of a text. I didn't check it until I was completely done with everything that I had to do. I went over to my dresser and grabbed my brass knuckles, gun, pocketknife, and taser. I stuck everything at the bottom of my purse and hung my mace on my key ring.

Ding...

My phone went off again. That reminded me that I never checked the first text. Jogging over to it, I checked to see who it was.

228-238-8127: Hi bu2ful. Can't wait 2 c u.

228-238-8127: This my numba. Save it sexy.

Me: Yep. Headed your way now. 😉

"I'm ready," Mone't announced when she stepped back inside the room.

"Cool. Here's a twenty for gas. Follow me in your car so he won't suspect anything by us riding together." That was my way of thanking her in advance.

"Girl, I don't want your damn money," she said and tossed the money back to me. I shrugged my shoulder, and we exited the house.

Traffic was a little bad going down Highway 90 to get to Ocean Springs. I was sure it had everything to do with people trying to get off and get home from work. It didn't bother me because it gave me a little more time to think about what I was going to do. Javonte's ass was going to give me some answers about why the hell his page suddenly disappeared. It took us about thirty minutes to get to the restaurant. We passed two accidents en route there. That explained why the traffic was so bad.

Mone't shot me a text and asked was I good when we pulled inside the parking lot. I texted her back and told her I was fine. I told her that Javonte' was standing in front of the restaurant. The fact that he was indeed the man in the pictures made me feel a little better. But I still wanted answers on what happened with his profile. I didn't like that. It almost made it look as though I was crazy trying to show someone something and it wasn't there.

Parking my car in front of the restaurant, I noticed that Mone't parked over to the side. That was fine with me in case he could recognize her from my pictures as well. I checked my makeup and hair one more time before I got out of the car. I nodded my head at Mone't to signal to her that I was fine as I made my way up to Javonte'.

"Hey, sexy lady," Javonte' greeted me. I extended my hand to shake his, but he had other plans. He pulled me in tightly and wrapped his arms around me. That nigga was strong as a fuckin' ox.

"Hey, Javonte'. How are you?" I asked, pulling myself away.

"I'm great. I'm so glad we finally got to meet. Aren't you?"

The smile that was once on his face faded. Nervousness started to set in, and I began to feel as though this wasn't a good idea after all.

"Ummm... Yeah. It was about time that we made this happen," I lied. I was ready to run. Something didn't feel right at all.

"Cool. You ready to eat."

"Yeah. I'm starving," I lied again. Too many negative thoughts were running through my mind for me to want to eat anything.

"Let's go then," he said and placed his hand on the small of my back. We were preparing to walk inside the restaurant before he stopped to look at me.

"What's wrong?"

"You don't seem to be feeling this. You're not even dressed for a date. How about we go do some goofy golf or bowling instead," he suggested.

"Are you sure?" I asked. I wasn't even sure why I asked that shit when I was ready to cancel this entire so-called date.

"I'm positive. I want you to be as comfortable as possible around me. Come on. Let's go. You can ride with me," he offered.

"I can drive. That way I can go home as soon as we are done, and you don't have to worry about bringing me back to my car. I'm not trying to be an inconvenience."

"You could never be an inconvenience to me, sweetie," he tried to reassure me. I didn't give a damn how nice he was being; something still didn't feel right with me. However, my dumb ass still wanted answers, so I agreed to go with him. I checked the parking lot to make sure Mone't's ass was still out there before I moved any further. I felt a lot better when I saw her.

We got to his car, and he played around with his door. For some reason, his passenger-side door wouldn't open.

"You want me to slide in from the driver's side or something?" I asked.

"No. Do you mind sitting in the back seat?" he asked.

"You mean like a child?" I replied. He had me fucked up. I wasn't no damn child being chauffeured around by my parent.

"No. Like I'm driving you around in a limo," he stated. "Be positive about it," he added.

"Fine." I rolled my eyes and slid in the back seat. He jogged around and got in on the driver's side. I reached inside my back pocket to take my phone out. It was gone. I knew I'd placed it back there when I got out of my car. "Have you seen my phone?" I asked Javonte'. He held it up in the air.

"Yeah, it was about to fall out of your pocket, so I grabbed it." I knew he was lying. That was the reason he hugged me. He saw me put my phone back there, and he had to get it away from me. He snatched it out of my pocket while he was hugging me. *Son of a bitch!*

"Hand it here, please."

"I'll hold on to it for now. I want to get your full, undivided attention while we are having fun. Is that a bad thing?"

"No. What's bad is me beating your ass if you don't give me my shit. Matter fact, let me out of this car. I'm not going anywhere with you. I reached for the door handle and tried to open it, but it wouldn't budge. The nigga had the fuckin' child lock on. That let me see that his ass was lying about the front door. It wasn't broken. He wanted me to think it was so that I could get my dumb ass in the back seat. He had this shit all planned out. He even had the damn window locks on so I wouldn't try to climb out.

"Naw. We 'bout to go have some fun. By the way, I want you to refer to me by my nickname from here on out. Nobody calls me Javonte'."

"What the fuck is your nickname? What the hell are you talking about?" I curiously probed.

"JC. Call me JC, baby," he informed me and zoomed out of the parking lot.

15
KAYSON

The very next day, I was sent to have the biopsy performed. We learned that I didn't have cancer. What I had was called pulmonary artery aneurysm. This was an outpouching in the arteries that travel from my heart to my lungs. It appeared as a mass when they completed my imaging tests. It was something that could have been fatale, but the doctors caught it in time to repair it by doing a surgical procedure known as an endovascular stent graft. I'd been in the hospital since it was done, and I was more than ready to go home.

Kyson came to the hospital each and every day to check on me. Sometimes he would bring the kids with him. He was still dealing with the courts and trying to maintain custody of them. I admired the fight that he'd put up to keep them. That said a lot about his character. Mone't came with him sometimes too. Not once did either of them bring up Toccara. I hadn't heard from her since the day I asked her to leave the hospital. That was confirmation enough that we were done. It was hard for me to deal with the first few days, but I quickly got over it. It wasn't like I really had any other choice. I wasn't the type of nigga that chased anybody. I replaced their asses. So many occasions, I told myself that Toccara was different and I needed to go out of my way to make her mine again. She proved me wrong each and every time.

Knock... Knock...

Not expecting any visitors since Kyson wasn't coming back until later, I didn't respond to the knock. I figured it was the hospital staff coming in to check on me. I kept my eyes on the TV the entire time.

"Kayson." Hearing her voice, my eyes darted from the TV over to the door where she stood. "How are you doing?"

"What are you doing here, Bree?" I asked her. I knew I made it clear that I didn't want anything else to do with her.

"I heard what happened to you. I wanted to check on you. How are you?"

Bree wasn't the same Bree I was used to seeing. Everything about her was different. She wasn't dressed up the way she normally was. Her hair was all over her head and she had an odor to her. She wasn't close to me, but I could smell her ass from where she stood.

"I'm good. What are you doing here, Bree? What's going on with you?" I was really concerned with what was going on with her. My body was still a little weak from the procedure. Sometimes it was hard for me to breath. No matter how big or small the procedure is, anything dealing with your lungs was going to be hard to bounce back from. At least that was the case for me.

"Why?" she asked out of nowhere.

"Why what? What are you talking about?"

"Why couldn't you love me? I lost everything because of you. You have everything and I have nothing now." She began babbling and talking out of her head. Nothing that she said was making sense to me. It was hard for me to take her serious.

As she continued to talk, I used my eyes to locate the call button. I needed the nurse or someone to get in here because I didn't trust Bree's ass. With the shit she pulled on Mone't and all the issues she caused between Toccara and me, I didn't put anything past her. The button must've fell. It was nowhere to be found.

"You need to leave, Bree," I told her.

"Answer me and then I will go. All I want to know is why," she rebutted.

"I've told you why several times. You weren't what I wanted. I couldn't force something that wasn't there. We both would've been unhappy, and I probably would've been cheating on you. I didn't want that."

"You wouldn't have had to cheat. I would've allowed you to do your own thing. We could've had an open relationship if that was what you wanted. You know I would've done any and everything I could to please you. You still don't see that?"

"Bree, I don't want an open relationship. I want a relationship with one person. We all deserve that happiness. You need more than I can give you. More than I was willing to give you. I'm sorry if you were hurt behind this. It's not like I never told you that I didn't want a relationship with you."

It was tiring having to keep going through this same conversation over and over again. Everything about Bree was exhausting to me. She needed some type of psychological help. Help I couldn't give her.

"You love me, Kayson. I know you do," Bree stated. She started walking toward my bed. I sat up and began searching for the button again. I didn't trust her ass. When I located the button, I pushed it repeatedly until someone answered.

"May I help you?" a woman came over the intercom and asked.

"I need security in here," I hollered back.

"No, he doesn't. Baby, stop playing," Bree loudly spoke. She continued on her journey toward me.

"Bree, get the hell back. Don't come near me," I warned her. "Aye, send security in here right now," I loudly spoke through the intercom.

My strength wasn't where I wanted it to be, but it was

enough for me to snatch the cord for the call button out of the wall. I stood from the bed and prepared myself to wrap it around Bree's neck. She acted suspect. I was going to hurt her before I allowed her to hurt me.

"Bree, get back," I ordered her once more. She still wasn't listening. She kept moving toward me. Bree picked a pillow up off the bed and started walking around it to get to me.

"Let's go home," she said. "Dear God, we are ready. Amen," she called herself praying.

"Dear God, that bitch lying. Take her and leave me here," I said a prayer of my own. Bree had me fucked up. She was wishing death on me with her weird ass. Security nor any of the medical staff had made it inside the room.

"He's going to do her the same way he did me. Toccara is not safe," she said out of nowhere. I didn't know what she was talking about.

"Bree, what are you talking about? You need help. Let me help you," I offered.

"Tell me you love me, Kayson. Tell me that I'm the only person you want to be with," she pleaded.

"I love you, Bree. You're the only one I want," I lied. If that was what I needed to do to get her out of my room, then I was going to do it. I had to figure out what she was talking about in regard to Toccara too. However, I knew I couldn't come out and ask her because she was going to shut down. Anything involving Toccara was a trigger for her, so I had to be smart about things.

"I knew you did. She was never good enough for you. It was always me. Let's get married. We can have kids and have the big family you always wanted," she concluded.

Bree got close up on me. My breathing started to become shallow. It had everything to do with my anxiety being all over the place. I needed to sit down. This was too much for me.

"Is everything okay in here?" Security finally came through the door.

Bree pulled out a knife and began swinging it at me. My body stung with each time she swung the knife and connected with any part of my body, mainly my arms. Using the cord that was still in my hand, I was able to wrap it around Bree's neck. Pulling it as hard as I could, I was trying to take her ass out. She had to go before she killed me.

"Let her go. Let her go now," one of the security guards ordered me.

"You let her cut your ass up and tell me if you'd let her go," I seethed. "This bitch not about to kill me."

"She's not. The police have been called. We've got it from here."

"She doesn't need to go to jail. She needs to go to the top floor. Something is wrong with her mentally," I told him.

"We understand that. Killing her won't help her," he advised me.

"Like hell if it won't. It'll take her out of her misery," I replied.

"What the hell is going on?" Kyson came running inside the room. His eyes damn near bulged out of his head when he saw the position I was in. "What the fuck! Let her go, Kayson. Killing her is what she wants you to do. She's still trying to ruin your life and you're about to let her. Don't give her that power. Let her go and let the police handle it," Kyson tried reasoning with me.

"I'm tired of her. I'm sick of the bullshit she's put me through. She made me lose Toccara."

"This isn't going to bring her back to you. We can work on getting Toccara back, but not if you kill Bree. You think Toccara is going to stand by you while you're doing a life sentence because of Bree? Come on, Kayson. You know anything involving Bree is going to make Toccara run. Let Bree go and let the police handle this shit."

It took some convincing, but I finally decided to let her go. She dropped down to the floor as soon as I loosened my grip on the cord. Glancing down at Bree, I didn't recognize the woman before me. I couldn't believe that I'd even given her the chance to get close to me. Bree was never my type. She was convenient. That convenience had done nothing but caused me problems.

"Discharge my brother right now," Kyson yelled to the nurse.

"We can't. We need to look at his cuts. We also need to wait for the doctor to come in and say that he can leave. She won't be back until in the morning," the nurse said.

"Fuck that! You couldn't keep my brother safe. How the hell did this nutcase get in here anyways? You were supposed to be watching him." Kyson was spazzing out on them.

"I'm sorry, sir. This is a hospital. We can't control who comes in and out of here. We didn't know anything about him needing security or we would've made sure he had it. Nothing like this has ever happened before," the nurse tried explaining.

"Fuck that shit! Y'all can't protect my brother. How the hell did y'all even know to send someone in here anyway?"

"I called them and told them that I needed security," I informed him.

"And how the hell long did you have to wait before someone came?" he asked.

"It had been a little minute," I admitted. "Calm down, bro. It's not their fault. They didn't know. Let them get me cleaned up and we can talk about what needs to happen after that."

"Fuck!!!" Kyson snarled before punching the wall. "Everybody get the hell out unless you're the nurse," Kyson ordered. People began scattering like roaches. Kyson didn't try to hide the fact that he was pissed. Shit, I was too. However, we couldn't blame the staff for what happened. Nobody knew that Bree was as unstable as she was or that she was going to come in and try to kill me. If that was what she was trying to do. All I could do was hope that she would be able to get the help that she needed.

"I love you, Kayson. I always have and I always will," Bree told me as she was being cuffed and taken out of the room.

"Stay the hell away from my brother. If I see you near him

again, I'm going to kill you myself," Kyson promised her. He said exactly what I was thinking.

The nurse took her time patching me up. She told me that all of the cuts I received from Bree were superficial and easily treated. They weren't deep so I didn't need any stitches. Steri-strips was what she used to seal the wounds. She tried talking to me to convince me to stay at the hospital until I saw the doctor, but I didn't want to be there. I couldn't spend another minute being away from my bed and not feeling safe. It made me wonder if Bree was the one who knocked me out and caused the fire at the pharmacy. It had to have been her. She was the only person that had it out for me.

"You ready?" Kyson stepped back in the room and asked.

"Yeah. Let's go. I'm sick of being here anyway," I responded.

"What about your medications? You really should wait until the doctor comes in the morning," the nurse suggested. By the time she'd finished her statement, Pops appeared in the room.

"What the fuck is going on in here?" he asked. Kyson and I explained everything to him. He shook his head and asked where Bree was. When we told him, he asked the nurse if the police were coming up to the hospital. She explained that since the hospital was considered private property, the Pascagoula Police Department wouldn't be coming up there but that they could put security on my room. Pops didn't like it but said that I needed to stay there until the doctor came. He didn't want me leaving until the doctor really checked me out and made sure I had all the prescriptions I needed. Although I hated to admit it, he was right.

Ring... Ring...

Kyson's phone started ringing. He glanced down at it and smiled. I knew that it had to be Mone't calling him. That was the only time that nigga really smiled. When it came to her and the kids, his ass always displayed this big ass Kool-Aid smile.

"I'm going to step out and get this. I'll be right back," he told us.

Pops sat in the room doing his best to convince me to stay. I didn't want to spend another night in that hospital. Bree popping her ass up there was all the sign I needed for me to know it was time for me to get the hell out of there. However, Pops was not planning on letting me leave. He even said that he was going to stay there with me. That was something I didn't want to happen because I knew his ass was going to try to treat me like a baby. I was a grown ass man and he needed to treat me as such.

"I gotta go. I'll be back when I can. I love you, bro," Kyson popped in the room and said before running out of there like he was headed to put out a fire. He didn't tell us anything. Pops and I knew something was wrong.

"Are you going to call him, or should I?" I asked Pops.

"No! Let him handle whatever it is. If he wanted us to know what it was, he would've told us. All I want you to do is get in the bed and rest. You've been through a lot tonight and I don't want you having any setbacks because of it. I promise I'm going to get you out of here tomorrow," Pops assured me.

"You really don't have to stay here," I advised him.

"Boy, shut your ass up. I'm not going anywhere. You're my son and I love you. No matter how old you get, you and your brother will always be my babies and I'm going to take care of you as long as I have air in my lungs. Now, get some rest," he suggested.

Pops took a seat on the sofa that was in my room. That was after he moved it around to where it was damn near blocking the door. He had them get someone from security to stick around outside my room. Bree was gone but I didn't put shit past her. As far as we knew, her ass could've been working with someone else. One thing she said bothered me. She kept saying something about Toccara not being safe. I didn't know what she was talking about, but I was determined to find out.

16

KYSON

Hearing that Bree was able to get to my brother and cause him more harm upset me more than anyone could imagine. Where the hell was hospital security? Then for him to tell me that he called for help before she cut him, and it took them a while to get to him pissed me off even more. He could've been killed. The thought of it was sickening. They were going to pay for almost causing me to lose my brother by their poor response time. Kayson wanted to be nice and say it wasn't their fault, but they needed better damn security.

Seeing that Mone't was calling made me feel a lot better. She was always my calm during the storm. All I wanted to do was crawl in the bed and lay under her. I answered the phone to see where she was and to tell her to get to the house. I had to put my request on hold when I heard how panicked she was.

"Hey baby," I answered the phone.

"She needs help!" she blurted out.

"Calm down. What are you talking about, baby? Who needs help?"

"Toccara. Somebody has her," she told me.

"What? What are you talking about? You aren't making any sense," I informed her. "Hold on. I'm going to call you right back." Pops was at the hospital with Kayson, so I was okay with leaving him there. Pops would never let anything happen to him. I had to rush out of the room with them and out of the hospital to find out what Mone't was talking about. Kayson had already been through enough so there was no way I was going to tell him what had happened without having all the information that I needed.

As soon as I slid behind my steering wheel, I connected my phone to my car radio and called Mone't back.

"Baby, what's going on?"

"Toccara came out on a date with some guy named Javonte' that she met online."

"When did she meet this guy?"

"She said it was a few weeks ago and they had been talking all the time. She felt like something was up because they made plans to meet tonight and when she got ready to show me his profile, it had been deleted."

"Then why the hell did she go out with him anyway?" The more Mone't talked, the more I thought back to when we were at the hospital with Kayson last week. The Javonte' guy had to be whom Toccara was talking to and doing all that smiling and shit for. I knew I was right in thinking she had been talking to someone else. "Where are you?" I interrupted Mone't and asked.

"We are driving down Highway 90. He is heading toward Gulfport. I'm following behind them," she advised me.

"Have you called the police?" I quizzed. If anything, that should've been the first call she made. She was putting herself in a dangerous position by following them.

"No, I called you. I didn't know what else to do. You're always the first person I call when something is going on," she admitted. It felt good that she trusted me enough to make me her first call in the event of an emergency, but the police were who she really needed to call.

"Mone't, baby, I need you to call the police. Call them on three-way," I advised her.

"Hold on," she told me. I heard her phone click and then I heard her pushing buttons.

"9-1-1, what's your emergency?" the dispatcher came over the phone and asked.

"My friend went on a date with some guy she met online. He threw her in the car with him and took her. She's trying to get out, but he won't let her. Please help her!" Mone't cried through the phone.

"Okay, ma'am. How do you know all of this?" the dispatcher asked.

"Why the fuck does that matter? She is telling you that her friend needs help. Get them sorry ass cops out to where she is NOW!" I yelled through the phone.

"Sir, I need you to calm down. Who are you?"

"I'm her boyfriend. She called and told me what was going on. I told her to call y'all. You are asking all those damn questions when you should be sending someone to help her," I grunted. It was frustrating as hell the way the woman was asking all of those questions instead of sending help.

"Sir, I need to get a little more information, so I'll know where to send help. Can you tell me what you see?" the dispatcher asked.

"I see the casino." Of all the things for her to say, she had to say that. She could've at least said the name of the damn casino considering there were a few of them in the area.

"Which casino, Mone't?" I probed.

"Please be quiet, sir. I don't need you to upset her. I need her to remain as calm as she can so that we can try to get to them," the dispatcher advised me.

"Track the fuckin' phone and you'll be able to find her with no problem. Who hired you? They must've put an ad in the newspaper for dummies," I bellowed.

"Sir, there is no need to be rude."

"And there is no reason to be dumb."

"Kyson, stop! You're making this worse. Please let me talk to her," Mone't whined.

"Fine." I was about to hang up the phone on her. How the hell was she going to tell me to be quiet when all I was trying to do was help her?

Doing as I was told, I shut the hell up. However, I wasn't going to be a sitting duck and let something happen to her. So, I opened my find my iPhone app and entered the iCloud information for Mone't's phone. As soon as it pinged her location, I pushed my pedal all the way down and headed her way.

17

TOCCARA

"I have her. Where do you want me to take her?" Javonte' was on the phone with someone. I remained quiet to see if I could make out who he was talking to. The sound of the voice sounded a little familiar. It was almost as if I'd been around it before, but not long enough to identify it out of the blue. "Fine. I'll be there in less than five minutes."

"Why are you doing this?" I asked once he ended the call. "You don't even know me."

"I know enough. I know that you hurt someone that I care about and now you're going to have to pay for it," he advised me.

"Javonte', what the hell are you talking about? We don't even know the same damn people. How the hell could I have possibly hurt someone you care about?" I was confused. Who the hell was he talking about? My mind wondered back to his Facebook page. We had five mutual friends. None of whom I had any personal relationship with other than knowing them from around the way. None of this was adding up.

A few minutes later and we were pulling up at some house in Gulfport. Peeking around, I surveyed my surroundings to see if I could spot anything that was familiar to me. The one thing I did see was a car that I'd seen a million times. It belonged to

LeBron. *What does he have to do with this?* I thought. Was he the reason that Javonte' had come after me?

"Get out of the car. If you scream, I'm going to shoot you," Javonte' warned me. We got out of the car with him screwing a silencer on the end of his gun. The house was immaculate on the outside. If it looked that good on the outside, I could only imagine how the inside would look. It didn't take me long to find out. With the gun poking me in the back, Javonte' led me up the three stairs leading to the inside of the house. He twisted the doorknob and pushed the door open. My eyes landed on a big ass portrait of LeBron and his wife. My mouth dropped.

"Take her into the living room," a female's voice spoke. It was the same voice I heard on the phone.

"Keep walking," Javonte' stated, pushing me further in the house with the gun still poking me in the back.

Slowly, I moved through the corridor of the house and into the living room. I stopped abruptly when I spotted LeBron tied to a chair in the middle of the floor.

"What you stop for? Aren't you going to do anything to save the man that you love?" his wife asked prior to walking around the corner with a gun in her hand as well.

"That's your husband. You're the one who needs to save him," I advised her. Shit, I wasn't checking for LeBron so her bringing me here was pointless. I wasn't about to lose my life trying to save him.

"He was my husband until he met you. All those other bitches knew how to fall in line. You had to be the one to make things complicated."

"Girl, fuck you! I didn't even know you existed. As soon as I found out about you, I told your husband to stay his cheating ass away from me."

"He filed for divorce. He left me because you wouldn't have anything to do with him. Do you know how embarrassing that is?" She aimed her gun at me. Tears relentlessly fell from her eyes. How the hell was she blaming me for what happened between her and LeBron? He was the one that hurt her, not me.

LeBron sat bound and gagged to the chair. He was no help at all. That was nothing new. Since she had him tied up, I figured she wasn't going to do anything to him. She was out for blood. My blood. If she wanted to do something to him, she would've done it by now.

"You see this shit, LeBron. This was the bitch you chose over me. I did everything for you. I was the one who took care of you when you were sick. When your credit was fucked up and you needed money, I was the one taking out the loans to help you save face. When your business was failing, I was the one begging people to take you on as a client. I did that. Not her. ME!" she screamed.

"Yeah, she did that. Not me. That's why this needs to stay between the two of you," I intervened.

"Shut up, bitch! I didn't ask for you to cosign anything for me."

"Don't call me another bitch. I'm not the one who cheated on you or left you. I don't know why the hell you are coming after me. I left him alone," I asserted to her. She needed to be taking her anger and frustrations out on him. I was not about to be her punching bag.

"BITCH!" she spat.

"I said don't call me out of my name again. You don't know me like that."

"Bitch... Bitch... Bitchity Bitchhhhhhh..." she sang, taunting me.

"You're going to make me fuck around and knock the edges back on your damn head. Fight me one on one. What do you need a gun for?" I quizzed. "Come on, hoe. You talking all that shit. LeBron cheated on you because you were weak. What man do you know wants to be with a weak-minded woman? You can't even think for yourself. Hell, if you wanted to hurt me, what did you need Javonte' for? You were too scared to do it alone. Ol' weak ass." I did my best to agitate her. One thing I learned about people was that they didn't think straight when they were mad. If I could get her madder than she already was, it would be easier for me to distract her and get the gun away from her. Or at least try to.

"Shut the fuck up!" She grabbed ahold of her head and spun around in a circle. She wasn't right in the head. Who the fuck would do that?

"You good, sis?" Javonte' asked her. He started walking over to where she was, and she lost it.

Pow... Pow... Pow...

LeBron's wife closed her eyes and began blindly shooting. I dropped to the floor and crawled behind the nearest sofa. You would've thought I was a soldier in combat.

"Get out of my head. Get out of my head!!" I heard his wife yelling. The shooting had ceased but I was still scared as hell.

Peeking around the sofa, I did my best to see if I could lay eyes on her. I couldn't think straight. I needed an escape plan. Suddenly, I could hear sirens nearing the house. It made me remember that Mone't had been following me. I was thankful I was smart enough to get her to come with me.

"We've got to go." I heard Javonte' say. His ass was sprawled out on the floor from ducking for cover. He stood up and grabbed LeBron's wife. He tried to pull her out of the door with him.

"Not until she's dead," LeBron's wife spoke.

"Fuck that! You're on your own. I'm not going to jail behind this shit. You told me you weren't going to hurt her. You've done nothing but caused me problems since you came back into my life. You had me help you set the fire at the pharmacy without telling me that someone was in there. You had me beating the shit out of the Bree's bitch ass because she was fuckin' Jared right along with you. Now this. I can't do this shit no more. I'm out," Javonte' announced. Everything was starting to make sense to me. Everything that had transpired was all because of LeBron's wife.

"You have to kill her. She can't live."

"Listen to yourself, Cherie. Your ass is about to go to jail. It won't matter if she's alive or dead, you still won't be able to be with LeBron. Either you can stay here and wait on them to arrest you or you can bring your damn ass on," Javonte' scolded her.

The woman who I now knew to be Cherie stood there contemplating her next move. The sirens continued to get closer and closer. Javonte' wasn't taking any chances. He dropped his gun and took off for the door. Cherie must've thought about it because she took off right behind him. When I could no longer see them, I scrambled through the house trying to find a phone. I needed to call Mone't to see where she was and to find out if the police were coming because of her. I had to get the hell out of that house. I didn't even bother to untie LeBron's ass. He was the reason we were in the situation we were in.

"Is there anyone else in here?" a deep voice yelled inside the house.

Not sure who it was, I hid behind a wall until I could see someone. The police came charging inside the house checking to see if it was all clear. Feeling safe, I came from around the wall and told them who I was.

"Toccara! Toccara, where are you?" Mone't's voice rang throughout the room but I didn't see her.

"Mone't?" I called out to her.

"Bitch, where are you?" she asked, as I stepped back inside the living room. I wondered how her ass even got inside the house.

"Mone't, didn't I tell your baldheaded ass to stay outside and wait for the police to let you know everything was clear before you ran in here? What if someone would've shot you?" Kyson came jogging inside, fussing at her.

"Then I would've been a shot ass," Mone't snapped.

"You ain't got to worry about them shooting you because I'm going to do it with your smart-ass mouth," Kyson voiced.

"Shut up, Ky. You always got to be an asshole. I had to make sure my friend was okay."

Mone't and Kyson stood there going back and forth with each other. I didn't want to hear the shit, so I walked off. LeBron's ass was still tied to the damn chair. I made my way over to one of the officer's and asked if she could give me a ride home. Of course, she told me I was going to have to go with them to answer a few questions. No matter what happened, I felt like I couldn't get a damn break.

Sitting outside on the steps, I waited for the police to clear the scene so they could take me to the police station. They tried to have me checked by AMR, but I declined because there was nothing wrong with me. LeBron eventually came walking out of the house as if nothing happened. He took a seat beside me on the steps.

"I'm sorry, Toccara," was the first thing he said to me, breaking the silence that was once between us.

"Thank you," I replied. He prepared to say something else, but I threw my hand up to stop him. There was nothing more he could say to me. I stood from where I was once sitting and walked away without looking back.

EPILOGUE
TOCCARA

SIX MONTHS LATER...

"Are you sure you want to do this?" my sister, Olivia stood in my room asking me.

"Yes. It has to be done," I replied to her.

Movers moved throughout the basement loading all of my belongings unto the U-Haul.

"Bitccchhhh..." Mone't stepped inside the house, yelling.

"Watch your damn mouth, Mone't," my mother told her.

"I'm sorry. I didn't know you were down here," Mone't informed my mother before giving her a hug.

"Do the two of you ever greet each other without using the word, bitch?" my mother queried.

"Nope," Mone't and I looked at each other and answered in unison.

"I stopped by to make sure everything was okay. Kyson and I are on our way to the courthouse," she announced. "Are you coming?" Not only was today the day of my big move, it was also the day that Kyson and Mone't were going to adopt Tamale' and Blaze.

Mone't played the recording for Estelada of what happened when they went out to eat. She confronted the so-called family members and Blaze's father about the recording. It turned out that the man claiming to be Blaze's father, Stan, was never even his father. The DNA test came back a few days after they went to eat. With him out of the picture, Kyson was free and clear to keep Blaze. However, he still had to fight for Tamale'. He was determined to not separate the two. Ultimately, he ended up giving her family members fifty thousand dollars in exchange of them signing papers stating that they would never come after her again. It was a lot of money, but it was all worth it in the end.

"Hellooooo... Do you hear me talking to you? Are you coming to the courthouse or not?" Mone't asked, removing me from my thoughts.

"Yeah. As soon as they finish loading everything on the truck, I'm heading that way."

"Cool. See you soon," Mone't stated and gave me a hug. She waltzed out of the room. I was proud of my friend. She'd come a long way. She made up in her mind that Kyson was who she was going to spend the rest of her life with. Since the kids were going to be a part of his life, she made it a point to let him know she was in it for the long haul as well. She told him that she wanted to adopt them along with him so they would be as much of hers as they were his. She was ecstatic when he agreed. That was great for them. She didn't want to be a mother at first, but it turned out, she was an even better mother than she thought she'd ever be. Especially, since the children had let their guard down and allowed her to build a relationship with them.

My mother and sister stayed to make sure everything in my room that needed to be in a box was in one. After a while, they told me they were going to take a break. Everything was pretty much out of the house anyway, so I was fine with that. They went upstairs to grab something to eat while I walked through the basement one last time to make sure I had everything that I was taking with me. I stepped back inside my room and began placing the things inside my duffle bag that I was going to need to get through the night.

Knock... Knock...

"Come in," I said, never looking up from what I was doing.

"Hey!" Kayson stated. That caused me to glance up at him. Our eyes locked and there was a tingling sensation running through my body.

"Hi," I replied to him.

"How have you been?"

"I've been good? How 'bout you?"

"I've been good as well. I mi-"

"Don't," I told him. I didn't want to hear any of it. It would only complicate things between us and I didn't want that.

"Toccara, I-"

"Stop Kayson!" We haven't spoken in months. That was the best thing for us."

"I don't believe that."

"You don't have to believe it. I know that it was. If we would've still been talking, we would've been fighting. We are now at a place where we can be in each other's presence without causing a scene. Let's start there," I told him.

Kayson and I hadn't seen or spoken to each other since the night I left the hospital. Both Kyson and Mone't respected me enough to not bring him up to me and I appreciated that. I appreciated the fact that he hadn't tried to reach out to me even more than that. It gave me enough time to reevaluate things. That was why I made up in my mind that it was time for me to have a fresh start.

"Where do we go from here?" he asked me.

"Friends. All I want to do is be friends. If something grows from that then so be it. I'm not going to force anything," I asserted. "Can you handle that?" I asked.

"Yeah." He dropped his head. I knew he didn't like what I

said but he had no choice but to accept my decision. Especially if he wanted me to be a part of his life.

It was hard for me to turn away from Kayson because I do believe he is a good man. He didn't cheat on me, but his actions still left me hurt. There was a lot of healing all of us would have to do behind the things that transpired over the past few months.

Bree didn't end up going to jail for what she did. That was due to Kayson going to court and speaking up on her behalf. I read about it in the paper. She was given time that she had to spend at the Mississippi State Hospital. That was probably the best place for her. Especially considering everything that she'd gone through. Javonte' and Cherie (LeBron's wife) were arrested the night they tried to kidnap me. They both received fifteen years. Where LeBron was, I didn't know. He never showed up for their court hearing. It didn't bother me though. If I never heard from him again, I'd consider it a blessing.

"I guess I'll be going then," Kayson told me.

"Take care. I'll see you around," I informed him.

"If you ever decide you want to come back to work, let me know. Since I won a settlement against the city for the officer pulling a gun on me that night, I used it and my insurance money from the fire to re-open the pharmacy. It's in a bigger and better location," he advised me.

"I'll keep that in mind," I responded and winked as he exited out of the room. It wasn't long before Olivia reappeared.

"Are you staying here tonight?" Olivia asked me.

"Naw. I need to get on the road," I replied.

"Toccara, your ass is moving to Pascagoula. There's only a damn street separating Pascagoula and Moss Point," she commented.

"And? I want to go home." I giggled.

It was true, I wasn't going far, but it was better than being in my parent's basement. I'd be experiencing real freedom for the first time. It was going to be a big change for me. Especially, since I'd be making the move on my own. It was bittersweet. But out of everything that happened, I promised myself that I was going to do whatever I had to do to avoid another bitch coming to me and letting me know that my so-called bae was creepin' with them.

THE END